MINNIE AND THE MANATEES

MARLENE BAIRD

This book is a work of fiction. Places, events, and situations in this story are purely fictional. Any resemblance to actual persons, living or dead, is coincidental.

© 2004 by Marlene Baird. All rights reserved.

No part of this book may be reproduced, stored in a retrieval system, or transmitted by any means, electronic, mechanical, photocopying, recording, or otherwise, without written permission from the author.

First published by AuthorHouse 08/30/04

ISBN: 1-4184-2686-5 (Paperback)

Printed in the United States of America
Bloomington, IN

This book is printed on acid free paper.

ALSO BY MARLENE BAIRD

MURDER TIMES TWO

THE FILIGREE CROSS:
THE SALVATION OF LARRY BROADFELLOW

DEDICATION

For Dad

Don't look back to count our tears
Except to measure your value
By their number

1993

And Mom

For countless lessons at your knee
For comfort, hugs and love
For being there

2003

NOTE FROM THE AUTHOR

Two hundred and fifty-one statute miles above earth, Astronaut Daniel Barry grips a handrail on the side of shuttle Discovery's cargo bay. Endless blue sky, muddled with streaky white clouds, yawns before his floating, boxy form. He and teammate Patrick Forester are installing a spare container of ammonia on the outside of the International Space Station. If it should be needed, this six hundred pounds of ammonia would be used to re-supply the space station's cooling system. Shuttle Commander Scott Horowitz is assisting the two space walkers by guiding Discovery's robot arm to the point of attachment.

The crew had blasted off from Kennedy Space center on Friday, August 10, 2001, prepared for the twenty-fifth space walk in International Space Station history. Just one month and a day later, on September 11, the United States became a different place. Space-walking and other incredible accomplishments paled as we faced our mortality.

Minnie and the Manatees was half-finished on that day when we all aged prematurely. When I returned to writing this book I found the tone softening, the characters behaving with more kindness. As they told their story I was reminded that, in all times, the human touch—the giving and receiving of tenderness—can heal.

MINNIE AND THE MANATEES

1

Gasping for air, Minnie lunged at the metal post which anchored the chain link fence, gripping it with both hands. Her quivering legs could not have carried her another fifteen feet. The fishy smell of the waterway mingled with that of her own pungent sweat. There was not a hint of breeze from the gulf, and the humid air of the South Florida night offered no relief. Her matted hair prickled under a woolly cap and she rubbed the side of her head against the pole to relieve the itching, wondering what on earth had come over her. The riskiest thing she had done in her life to that point was wearing shorts and a halter top on her forty-fifth birthday.

A half-hour earlier, while dressing all in black, her mind had spun with anxiety. As she stuck the kitchen knife into her pants pocket she felt like a cat burglar, except that they were slim, agile people who knew karate. She was a fifty-seven-year-old divorcee who had gained thirty pounds since learning about her cheating husband.

While her legs recovered from the run, she checked the sky and saw that the waning moon cooperated, staying behind thick clouds. A single bulb dangled high over the entrance to the marina. Though no more than forty watts in strength, it seemed to expose her like a floodlight in a jail yard, and Minnie knew she could not stay there long. She allowed herself a couple more deep breaths then reached for the tumbler lock. Now, the darkness was against her; it was almost impossible to see the small numbers.

"Damn," Minnie whispered. She seldom cursed but this seemed to be the night for breaking patterns. She recalled another thing about cat burglars: they don't need reading glasses. Squinting, Minnie slanted the lock this way and that under the meager light. Even though it had been over a year since that boat ride with the Castleburys, she recalled the combination. They had explained that the condo association changed the marina code every January first but they kept it simple. It was the four digits of the current year, backwards. Minnie found the number one and the zeros by feel. She rolled them to the center line. After only two misses she found the number two. The lock clicked open.

Hunched over almost double, thighs burning, Minnie crept along the dock. Jimmy Simm's boat, built solely for speed, hunkered low in the water. There was a cabin cruiser moored on one side and a lofty fishing boat, complete with satellite dish, on the other. Its size provided Minnie some protection from any insomniacs who might be standing behind darkened condominium windows.

At close range Simm's boat looked wide and firm, so Minnie thought it would be stable. But when she stepped down the boat responded to her weight and shifted away from the dock.

She cried out before she could clamp her mouth shut. Her legs were spreading apart, one foot on the dock, one on the boat. She flung her body forward and fell onto the hull. Splayed on the slick surface, she stayed still for an agonizing few minutes expecting to see lights pop on and hear doors squeak open. But she heard only the slosh of water as the boat settled and the hum of a car several streets away.

Minnie felt her way past the seats and over a couple of duffel bags to the rear. Two huge engines loomed against the glimmer of the water. Taking the kitchen knife from her pocket, she felt for exposed screws which she hoped might be holding the motors in place. Her fingers traced inch after inch, foot after foot, of smooth fiberglass. If there were screws involved, they were buried. Why hadn't she studied a boating magazine and been better prepared? Too eager to act, she may have sabotaged herself.

Her groping fingers did find what seemed to be a gas cap on the outside edge of the boat. Looking for something to use as a scoop, Minnie unzipped one of the duffel bags and came up with a thermos. With its cup she dipped water and poured it into what she hoped was the gas tank. In the stillness, the sluicing noise seemed as loud as the rush of a stream. After a few well-spaced dips, Minnie replaced the cup and the thermos and sat back on her heels.

Searching for gas or water lines, she returned to the front of the boat and felt under what would be the dash if it were a car. She stretched her arms into the narrow space and felt two lines. She sawed at one of them with the serrated edge of the knife, but since she couldn't see anything beyond her elbows she had no sense of how much damage she was doing. She chose the other line and, after a couple of minutes of sawing, felt an abrasion begin to form. The line was coated with a braided fiber which was shedding and falling through her fingers. She felt the knife hesitate—it had gone through to the rubber. Flushed with success, she worked harder, perspiration soaking her long-sleeved T-shirt. When she felt a trickle of moisture on her fingers she grinned. Then she heard a car approaching fast.

Minnie scrunched down to a ball. The car stopped in front of the marina gate, brakes squealing. Minnie clamped her eyes shut as if to render the night even darker.

"You're a slimy pile of carrion fodder," a woman screamed. A car door slammed and high heels clicked on the pavement, moving in the opposite direction, toward the condominium building.

"Don't be so damned touchy," a man's voice called.

"Eff you!" she yelled, her voice catching as though tears would be next.

A window slid open. "Hey down there, it's three o'clock in the morning!" The window slammed shut, and the car sped off.

It was suddenly so quiet that Minnie heard her heartbeat in her ears. What a stupid idea this was; she could so easily be caught. She waited a full five minutes, then stepped out of the boat, crept along the dock, relocked the gate and ran.

2

It seemed no one else was awake yet. From her screened patio Minnie could see nothing but black windows in the condos across the waterway. She sighed, then placed a red nine on a black ten. She flicked the corner of the card with an oval fingernail, and it slapped against the tiled table. Since the game demanded so little attention, her thoughts wandered, again, to the question of whether she should go back to her maiden name. In thirty-three years of marriage to Antony she had hated having to say Minnie Zuccarelli. It sounded like a lesser Italian dish.

  Sighing again—an annoying habit born of the recent disquiet in her breast—she tucked a loose strand of Clairol-red hair behind the stem of her glasses then hoisted her bulk from the plastic chair. Its splayed legs drew together, squealing against the vinyl floor. She scuffed in bunny slippers to the edge of the patio and leaned her forehead against the cool screen, pressing a grid into her fair skin.

Minnie And The Manatees

Three buildings identical to her own, except for their preferred location on the gulf, sliced her view of the horizon into five sections. With the sun rising behind her, the buildings lightened from the top down. Then, as Florida tilted more eagerly toward dawn, the entire sky blushed. There was a time when such a glorious morning would have lifted her mood.

She turned off the patio light and looked straight down, studying the waterway six floors below. Private docks jutted into the strip of water. On her side of the canal modest pleasure craft were moored to wooden piers. On the other side, the big money side, each condo building had its own marina. Those larger boats warranted the chain link protection she had recently challenged. But Minnie wasn't looking at boats. She sought out rounded shapes beneath the water's surface.

A few weeks earlier, just before that adventure which had rendered her sleepless, she had seen a manatee and its baby gliding directly below her balcony. The bull-dog nosed, bulbous creatures slid effortlessly through the water. She watched them roll, gently rubbing against one another. The baby moved with complete leisure and abandon.

Minnie's spine straightened and all the old anger returned as she remembered the rest of that morning. Off to her right powerful motors had screamed into life, and within a minute the idiot driver sped past, his wash jostling all the boats. Jimmy Simm, of course. The condo association had first warned then fined him, then reported him to the authorities, but nothing affected the cocky twenty-seven-year-old. Cursing, Minnie had shaken both fists at him as he swept away to her left, out into the estuary. When he was out of sight, she redirected her eyes downward, searching the churning water for the manatees. They were gone. Did the mother have time to coax her little one deeper, to safety? Could that wavering dark stripe in the water be blood?

All that day her anger built. That night she paced for hours, then set out at three o'clock in the morning intent on damaging Simm's boat. The run along the waterway, with the kitchen knife bouncing against her thigh, could not have been longer than a half mile but seemed endless. She had run crouched down to shrink her silhouette, and the distance was lengthened by her seeking out shadows. She remembered the rasp of her breath being loud in the still night.

Minnie found she was gripping the lapels of her robe and panting, as if she were running again. She released the fabric and breathed slowly. If only she had simply cursed at Simm, and not acted. If she had contained her fury she would not be out on this deck every morning playing cards and pretending to enjoy the sunrise while fear constricted her throat. Fear that the next buzz of the doorbell would bring the police.

Suddenly it was no longer dawn, but day. During her musings the sky had bled of color and become steely. Only a few clouds would relieve the oppressive heat again today, and the gulf lay flat and leaden, as if garnering strength to support the thick, humid air.

Her eyes were drawn to a slim figure jogging along the waterway. The dark, bouncing pony-tail told her it was Catherine James, the real estate agent who handled sales for the condo developer. The sales office, which was a renovated, single-bedroom condo at ground level, had a full bath, so Catherine would run early in the mornings, then shower and change to her day clothes. Catherine's jogging efforts paid off; the woman had the figure and complexion of a model.

"I have to borrow your walkways," she had told Minnie. "Running in my own neighborhood is like going to a singles bar in a mini-skirt. It brings out all the dogs." But Catherine was being diplomatic in describing where she lived. Minnie knew the area, which was not safe, and the enemy would be two-legged. She wondered why Catherine stayed in such a run-down part of the city, but didn't think it proper to ask.

Minnie ran hands down her own softening thighs. The past few weeks she'd been too tired to attend the aerobics classes in the pool. Sleepless nights stole your days, too.

As Catherine disappeared around the corner of a building, Minnie peered straight down again. Dismissing shifting shadows in the water, she strained to see her manatees. "Come back," she whispered. "It's safe now."

The ringing phone pierced the morning air and Minnie ran inside to quiet it. It would be Antony; he, alone, knew of her tossing nights and panicky awakenings.

"Bad night?" he asked.

"Of course."

"Any luck this morning?" Meaning, had she seen any manatees.

"No."

"Be patient, they'll be back."

Minnie dropped her glasses to the countertop and rubbed the bridge of her nose. "Are you going out today?" she asked. Antony had worked for various fishing enterprises, and now did it solo, earning a few dollars to augment his retirement.

"Naw, I didn't sleep either. Maybe I'll just cruise up the river this afternoon. Give the gawkers something to look at."

Minnie pictured the tourists and school children who visited the Ford/Edison museum in Fort Myers, spotting Antony's fishing boat on the river. Florida was so populated with glistening white pleasure boats that sighting his dumpy tub, draped with aging poles, droopy lines and snaggled nets, would be like discovering a lost, exotic breed.

"Do you want to go to dinner this week?" he asked.

"Why don't you come here and we'll just order a pizza or something."

Minnie And The Manatees

"Sure." Some eagerness had gone out of his voice lately. Perhaps Antony had finally accepted that friendship was all he could expect with his meal.

After the divorce she thought she would probably never see him, but he had moved only a dozen miles from their condo, visited as often as she would have him, and called daily. The settlement had been simple. Neither Antony's fishing jobs nor her position at the bank had paid that much. Buying a condo on the waterway had been a major investment, but it had increased in value by more than two hundred thousand dollars since they purchased it. Even so, Antony had asked for little when he left. No doubt guilt-ridden, he took only the tool box, his Harley which had been out of commission for years, and the old car—his pink and chrome baby. On Friday afternoon, when he came for dinner, he would zip down Highway 41 in his 1959 Coup de Ville convertible. Minnie could imagine his still-dark hair flying, the car's fins slicing the air. He would arrive at her door with a smile and a bag of Hershey's kisses.

Antony replaced the receiver and contemplated his day. He had told Minnie he would probably go out on the boat but could not muster any enthusiasm. He ran the electric shaver carelessly over the stubble on his cheeks and chin. Pulling on yesterday's knit shirt and wrinkled khakis, he slid into deck shoes and walked a half block down the alley to the shack he rented for a garage. His apartment building provided only open parking, and the Caddy had never spent a single night under the stars.

His 1974 shovelhead Harley was nosed into a corner, barely leaving walking space between it and the car. Dust sat thick on the canvas drape. Since the motorcycle hadn't run in almost ten years and it would take a good chunk of his savings to get it back in shape, Antony tried to forget what he was missing.

A treated duster hung from a nail on the wall. He removed it from its plastic sleeve and ran it over the car's smooth body, making it gleam. Splintered boards protruded dangerously close to the sides of the car as he backed out, but an attempt to fix any one of them would probably flatten the entire structure. The weathered slats had settled into a design of their own, as delicate looking and as tough as a bird's nest. It had held through many a storm. He rolled the car over the gravel at seven miles an hour so that a pebble could not spurt up and strike the undersides of his fenders.

"Hey, Suzy," he called, pulling into Brew Heaven, the drive-through where he picked up his morning coffee. It was a converted camping trailer sheathed in battered aluminum, the trailer hitch sitting on concrete blocks. Two side windows had been joined to create the wide space through which Suzy passed the drinks.

An over-tanned forty-year-old face, softened by a fluff of prematurely silver hair, appeared. She smiled out at him. "It hasn't finished perking. You're early."

"I can wait," Antony said, shutting off the motor.

"Going fishing today?" Suzy asked, leaning her forearms on the stainless steel shelf. Antony remembered how thrilled she had been to find that shelf on the side of the highway. It fitted her window exactly and matched the walls of the trailer.

"Can't seem to get going this morning," he said.

She winked at him, a habit he had found endearing for about six months. "Been talking to Minnie?"

"Hmph," Antony grunted.

"You look like a puppy who has been shown his dinner, only to be led away. I recall you telling me you had finally moved on. Of course, that was at the beginning of our relationship when you might actually have believed it."

"Isn't that coffee ready?" Antony asked.

"I'll hear it when it's ready. I bumped into Holly the other day. We're considering starting a Zuccarelli's Ex Club. We could all get together once a month and commiserate."

"It's not that bad."

"All nice gals, too. You ever going to find the right one? I mean, the second right one?"

"I heard the pot gurgle. It's ready."

Suzy half turned, talking over her shoulder. "We thought matching ball caps, wouldn't that be cute? Couldn't decide on the logo, though." She traded him a large dark Columbian with a dash of cinnamon for two dollar bills. "If we charged dues we could easily raise enough money for a heck of a blow-out a couple of times a year."

She was still talking when Antony pulled away.

He drove aimlessly for a half hour, sipping at his coffee, ending up near the Fort Myers pier. He parked and carried his cup out to the end. Two sleepy fishermen with lines in the water nodded at him, and returned to staring at the flat, gray gulf. Antony draped himself over the wooden rail and watched the water break a few hundred feet away as a dolphin rose, then curled back beneath the surface. A second one followed. They reminded him of Minnie's manatee mother and her baby, which made him think about his own mother. He automatically made a sign of the cross. She had been in his thoughts more than usual lately; he felt her strong will pulling on him as sharply as if she had him by one ear. And he knew the reason: she would gasp if she could see how shabby and pointless his life had become. "Smart dressing is the mark of a smart mind," she would mutter when he was a kid, shoving him back toward his room to polish his shoes.

Antony, the youngest, was spoiled by his five sisters. Alice, Gabby, Marie, Antonia and Shirley had seldom approved of the girls he dated, but they immediately embraced Minnie. She was just seventeen when he first brought her home to meet the family. Gallons of tears had been shed at the wedding and even more when he moved her from Brooklyn to Florida. Yes, those siblings had loved him unconditionally, until the day they learned he had cheated on Minnie. Overnight he experienced the wrath of a disturbed sisterhood. It was akin to swinging a baseball bat at a hive of wasps, naked.

He dumped the last ounce of cooled coffee into the water and headed back to his car. Suzy was a smart-aleck, dishing out sarcasm with her coffee, but she was right; he'd dated far too many women in the last couple of years. His buddies always chided him about his fatal charm, and Antony had no explanation for the fact that women were readily attracted to him. He didn't realize that the attention from all those sisters had given him a great gift. They taught him to appreciate women. Even the smell of hair spray quickened his senses. He responded to slippery moods and quick tears, so women shared confidences with Antony they had not told their best friends. In short, he could have any number of them, but wanted only one.

3

All of the condominiums had been built to catch the prevailing winds; that is, they were faced in the right direction and there were no internal hallways. A person actually entered from the back of each building. After taking the elevator from the ground floor one stepped onto a painted cement and brick landing, walked along the landing to the appropriate door and entered the condo near the kitchen. Then, in the simplest layouts, such as Minnie's, the bedrooms and baths were on your right, the kitchen, dining and living areas on your left. Looking straight ahead, through the living room, one saw sliding glass doors which opened onto the deck. That is where Minnie stood when she was searching for her manatees, and that is where she was now, waiting for Antony's arrival. Her nervous state had her actually wringing her hands. In the morning she had learned some shocking news.

Even though his arrival was imminent, her mind was so muddled that when the doorbell rang

Minnie And The Manatees

she jumped. She ran to the door and opened it immediately, not doing her usual fisheye check.

Antony grinned at her and held out the sack of Hersheys.

"I've got three bags in the freezer now," Minnie said, taking them. She went into the kitchen and reached for a candy dish. She was glad of the opportunity to turn away from Antony. He had bought new slacks, the creases still sharp. His handsome, windburned face glowed, and, in spite of her preoccupation, she had felt a jolt of attraction when she opened the door. Would he never change? She used to want him to grow up, now she just wanted him to get old. Since the divorce her own hair had turned ashy beneath the treatments, and, after gaining so much weight, elasticized black capris with hip-covering shirts had become her uniform.

She dumped a handful of the candies into a dish that read, The Everglades, 1964. There was not much else left of that honeymoon trip. The candies covered the droopy alligator on the bottom, except for his tail, which trailed up and over the lip.

"I'm not going to eat these, you know," she said, offering him the dish. Because she was tense, her voice sounded false to her ears, but Antony didn't seem to notice. The article in the morning paper had shaken her to the core, and she had come close to calling off this dinner date. But as the day progressed she realized that one of things she still needed from Antony was emotional support.

He took one kiss and peeled away the silver foil. "You've changed your nail polish again. Is that brown?"

Minnie held up her free hand, fingers splayed. "Cinnamon Java. Reds are out of fashion." She noticed her hand shake and abruptly pulled it out of the air. She didn't want to tell Antony her bad news until after they ate, but, being so jittery, she wondered if she could actually wait that long.

"Do your clients like brown on their own nails?"

"Some will try anything new. A few make me use their favorite color week after week, but most are somewhere in between."

"Do you still like doing nails? Don't you miss the bank?"

Changing jobs was one of the things Minnie had done after the divorce in an attempt to establish herself as a new person. Antony seemed threatened by it, as if that foreshadowed other changes.

"I like most of my clients real well, but the best part is that I can almost set my own hours."

Antony moved further into the small kitchen. "What's this? Crab cakes, creamed peas and lemon meringue pie. You said to expect pizza." Then he grinned. "I know what this is about. You've won the lottery and refuse to share."

"I needed to be busy today," Minnie said. "Let's have a drink."

She poured iced-tea glasses full of Beringer's White Zinfandel 1999, and they moved to the sofa. Trying to perch daintily on the edge of a cotton cushion, Minnie made a toast. "To surprises."

Antony's eyebrows rose and his eyes twinkled. "I can't wait."

Minnie took a long swallow of wine, then another. "One thing we could always do was talk," she began.

"Oh, sweet, that's not all," he said earnestly. "We did almost everything well."

"Never mind. I guess you haven't seen the paper. No, you don't even get the paper. My mind is jumpy." She took another swallow.

"Easy. You're not that good a drinker."

"I've gotten better. Anyway, here." Minnie handed him the second section of the paper, pointing to a small article.

As he read, she watched Antony's color drain, his hand reach uncertainly toward the coffee table to deposit his glass. "They've recovered the body? Surely not."

Minnie took another gulp of wine.

"Why the hell didn't the sharks finish him off?" Antony asked of no one.

"Even a shark wouldn't like Jimmy Simm," Minnie said. An alcoholic giggle escaped her. Then she burst into tears.

She woke hours later with a stiff neck and a sour mouth. Her right arm and leg were pinned to the sofa by the weight of Antony's body. He snored, his head on the bulky armrest. The only light was a fuzzy glow from the kitchen clock. They had forced some dinner down, gone over the sketchy details of the article a dozen times, then he had held her as she cried.

Antony snorted and woke himself up. She felt his body tense as if he was uncertain of his whereabouts. "It's me," she said. "We fell asleep on the sofa."

"Oh, God," Antony moaned. "Did we finish off that awful bottle?" He sat up. "I must have crushed you."

He snapped on a table lamp and Minnie covered her face with her hands. "What time is it?" she mumbled between her fingers.

"Eleven-thirty."

Minnie rose from the couch, curling away from the light. "Well, you might as well stay over. I'll get some bedding."

"Min, if you're okay now, I'll go on home. After this nap I won't get back to sleep for ages."

"Whatever you like."

Standing, he put his arms around her again. "Try not to worry too much. We don't know what will happen next."

From the cement landing outside Minnie's kitchen door she could look down on the swimming pool and, further to the right, the visitor parking lot. She watched until Antony was safely away,

Minnie And The Manatees

then set a full pot of coffee to brewing. She pulled a shoe box from under her bed and removed one of two newspaper clippings. It had appeared just after her visit from the police. "Local Man Missing: Neighbors of James Simm, 27, were interviewed yesterday. . . ." She got a chill remembering the policeman sitting across the kitchen table questioning her. Her only advantage was that he had looked about twelve years old. She tried to convince herself he didn't have the experience to recognize her answers for the lies they were.

"How well did you know James Simm?" he had asked.

"Not well." *Actually, I avoided him whenever possible.*

"Were you aware of any of his habits, when he came and went, for instance?"

"No." *Only that he liked to race his outboard motor over innocent sea creatures.*

"Did you see him on the day of his disappearance?"

"No." *And he didn't see me, either. No one could have seen me on that moonless early morning.*

Minnie sighed so deeply that she shuddered. She read the next clipping, from a week later, though she knew every word by heart. Following a sudden and fierce storm, James Simm's boat had been found a dozen miles from shore, disabled, and speculation was that he'd probably been washed overboard and drowned.

Now, according to this morning's paper, they had found the body, no doubt bloated and stinking.

Tears welled as she picked up her scissors and carefully cut out the report. *I didn't mean for this to happen. I didn't mean to kill you.*

Minnie stashed her clippings in the box alongside the kitchen knife. She had intended to toss it into the water that awful night but tension had made her grip it hard, and she found herself back in her condo, panting, knife in hand. She couldn't return it to the cutlery drawer as it carried a slight knick which would be a daily reminder of her folly. But she hadn't tossed it in the garbage either. Was she like the criminal who needed to be caught?

She finished the last cup of coffee, then waited hours for the pink dawn. But morning offered only a slowly lightening gray, and the canal below, where she searched for her manatees, offered even less.

4

Catherine James's thick, black hair swept her shoulders as she brushed rhythmically, tossing it side-to-side. She interrupted her routine only for quick drags on her cigarette. 'Drop dead gorgeous,' Mike would say if he were with her, and not in Atlanta. On the nights when he could stay over, he always stood behind her as she completed her bedtime preparations, his robust body completely framing her in the mirror just as he wanted to protect her in real life. Mike had left on this last business trip in as foul a mood as she'd ever seen him, that is, he gave her only a mild kiss and a pat on the butt as he headed for the door.

After he picked her up at work, they had eaten Chinese, then come back to her place. No sooner were they in the door, than he suggested, again, that she move to a better place, in a better neighborhood.

"Stop it, Mike," she said, stepping out of the four inch heels she always wore. They were a hazard when showing prospective buyers the newer condo buildings which were still under construction, but she was not complete without them.

He smiled, advancing toward her. "Come on, Cat. This place is—"

She cut him off before he could hurt her feelings. "It's all I can afford, and it's mine."

This was not true. She could afford better. But Catherine was stuck in some time warp, unable to leave the house where she had grown up. And it didn't even hold happy memories. She could barely face the pathology of this herself, much less try to explain it to someone else.

Mike made his usual argument. "What difference who can afford what? I'll help you. You can have anything you want."

"Except respectability."

"Aw, Cat. Look at you." He stood close, his bulky hands on her hips. "You're so damn classy, looking you makes all the other women in this town wish they were half as respectable."

Catherine moved away from his hands. "I've told you a hundred times, I'll move when I make enough money to do it on my own. The high-end condos at Estero Shores hardly ever come on the market. I haven't had one decent place to sell in a couple of months."

She walked into the bedroom, unbuttoning her suit jacket. "The new buildings are so far from the waterway I have to tout the convenience of

Minnie And The Manatees

being closer to shopping. Even dummies can see through that."

Mike followed, pleading, "But you don't even have to—"

Catherine turned on him. "Yes, Mike. I do have to work. It's for me. Can't you get that through your thick skull?"

Still he smiled. "Maybe something will open up. Or you could go to work for someone else. I know people in Naples."

She glared at him, biting her tongue. That was when he gave her the virginal kiss and the pat on the behind. "Gotta go."

Catherine brushed more vigorously. Mike would give her anything she asked, but she told herself she had *some* standards. Loving a married man was about her limit.

She smoothed eighty-dollar-an-ounce wrinkle cream on her face and neck and plumped the pillows against the headboard of her sleigh-bed. It was the only elegant piece of furniture in the house. Two years ago Mike had it delivered while she was at work. His lavish gifts had seemed romantic before she equated his generosity with control.

Satin slithered as she rolled back pink sheets and the light-as-air comforter. She propped herself against the pillows and lifted her daily calendar from a bedside table. Every night, when she was alone, she used this time to plan her next day, to make sure she followed up on each legitimate lead her conversations with clients suggested. It had a page for every week, but the pages were only four by six inches, the daily squares not big enough to hold much information. A phone number was neatly written in the next day's square along with a name and the note, "one bedroom, cheap." She had nothing cheap to offer the woman but some of the newer units were one-bedrooms, and people had been known to lie about their financial status.

In this evening's square she noted, "Atlanta." A few months prior she had begun to mark down Mike's business trips. At first she had written, "Mike-Savannah-2" for two nights away. After a while the numbers became depressing, and she shortened it to "M-Jacksonville." Now, she simply noted the city, often abbreviated, and sensed that this growing distaste for detail foreshadowed a growing dissatisfaction with Mike.

Catherine put the calendar away and picked a newspaper off the stack on her comforter. She saved the cigarettes and the newspapers for when Mike was away. She would have loved for them to read the paper together, then discuss the news, but Mike had fixed ideas about everything. The space station was a waste of money. Crime statistics, bogus. Politicians, well, that was where his language became too much to bear. She dropped the paper to her lap. Why did she love him at all? Because he was strong; she felt safe with him. Because he made love to her as if no other woman had ever existed. And because he loved his son more than he loved her.

Adrian McCreary, a Down Syndrome child, had a smile Catherine had come to adore simply from photographs. Mike carried a half dozen of them in a special wallet, showing Adrian from infancy to his current fourteen years of age. All of the pictures were fingered to softness. When Mike looked at those pictures with such love, he became a superman in her eyes.

Now lonesome for him, Catherine read her newspapers with wandering interest, almost missing the article about the discovery of Jimmy Simm's body. Everyone had assumed he had drowned, but it was still a shock to have his death confirmed.

Where, exactly, had he lived? Catherine went to her desk and unfolded a map of the development. Building 2, on the water, top floor. It was one of the largest and priciest units, with two master bedroom suites and a balcony that ran its full length. He'd seemed like such a shiftless kid; how could he afford that particular condo?

Nosey by nature and profession, Catherine was well aware that Jimmy had no family who would want to move in. "Not that I'd ever ask, but my folks'll never come down here," he once told her. "Stubborn as jackasses" was how he'd described them, apparently oblivious to the power of genetics. "They think Chicago is the center of the universe. Can you imagine?" His freckled forehead had wrinkled in disbelief as he shook his head. Catherine remembered a time when she'd found his stocky build and confident manner slightly attractive, but that was before he'd suggested they go skinny-dipping some time.

"Do you have brothers or sisters?" she'd asked, wondering whether the sheer agony of living with him might have done them in.

"Naw. Just me. In a few years I'll inherit a couple of cars and a house that ain't been repainted in twenty years." He apparently assumed his folks were so decrepit they couldn't possibly live much longer.

Catherine shuffled through papers and business cards in her desk drawer. Just last week there had been a man from Denver who said he would be interested if a prime location became available. Scottish name, McKay. She found his card and turned it over. She had scribbled a note on the back: Serious, single, Johnston & Murphy loafers. Judging people by their shoes was an infallible way of separating real money from suggested wealth.

Catherine returned to her bed, business card in hand, calculating three things: how best to approach Jimmy's folks about her handling the condo sale, the time difference between Fort Myers and Detroit where Ronald McKay lived, and the commission on a sale of upwards of five hundred thousand dollars.

5

Marching with a half-dozen other women in the pool, wet to her midsection, Minnie pulled her legs through the water. The shadow of her building fell across the pool, eliminating the early sun, and the water held a chill. Only Antony's call this morning, insisting that she return to her exercise program for her own health, had forced her into the bathing suit which now pinched under her arms.

"More energy, ladies. More energy," the instructor shouted. "Pump those arms." Sylvia, the drill sergeant, was twenty-nine, slim, and completely dry since she conducted the class from the cement. Minnie trudged more deliberately and felt cellulite rippling on the backs of her thighs. If only it were being massaged away. "About turn, ladies." Maybe Sylvia actually had some military training.

When Minnie faced the deep end of the pool she shifted her eyes away from the diving board. It always brought to mind a picture of

Gregory Barnes floating in its shadow, facedown, arms outspread. Though Minnie had not actually seen his body, she had received so many detailed descriptions that the image haunted her for months. Gregory had been known as a poor swimmer and, because that embarrassed him, he often practiced in solitude. When his body was found dressed in swimming trunks, with his towel and keys lying on the pool deck, the police made a cursory investigation and ruled the death an accidental drowning. Probably gay and genuinely kind, he was popular with almost everyone, including the husbands.

"Minnie, stay with us," Sylvia demanded. A person couldn't even slow down to remember a good friend.

"Faster, ladies, faster. Longer strides."

Minnie attempted to show more enthusiasm, swishing her arms through the water, but she groaned when she saw Sylvia scoop up an armful of six-foot long noodles. Sylvia tossed one Minnie's way—a lime green snake made of foam. The idea was to make a saddle of the noodle, putting it between one's legs with one end coming up to the chest in front, and the other rising to the middle of the back. Because she was in only four feet of water, Minnie accomplished that. Sylvia moved along the lip of the pool waving them toward the deep end. "Come on ladies, move it, move it."

As always Marge Higgins, in full makeup and a lacquered hairdo, led the way. A former Olympic gymnast, she had no worries about

Minnie And The Manatees

tipping over. The other women didn't wear all their makeup to the pool, but Marge had never accepted that the cameras were no longer pointed her way. As if to garner even more attention, she was given to eccentric dressing. At one community potluck she wore pantaloons with a silk shirt and slippers that curled up at the toes. Another time Minnie had bumped into her at the mall. Marge looked like a gypsy, her thin frame draped in green velvet, with thick gold chains at the waist and around her neck.

The costumes alone were enough to make Minnie keep her distance, but there was a more compelling reason for Minnie's discomfort whenever Marge was near. Each time Minnie laid eyes on the woman she was reminded of Antony's faithlessness. Not that Marge was the other woman, thank goodness. Minnie felt she could not have survived if he had cheated with someone she knew.

"Minnie," Sylvia called out. "Are you with us?"

Minnie gripped the column of foam in front of her, strangling the innocent floater. Her toes stretched as she felt the bottom of the pool angling downward. When she could no longer touch, she froze. All the ladies passed her, their legs scissoring the water. Uncertain, Minnie slowly pushed her right leg forward and began to "walk" as the others were doing. Within seconds she was sideways in the water, the noodle lifting her left hip to the surface, the right half of her face submerged. She reached for the edge, just grasping the lip of the pool with her fingertips.

"Here," Sylvia said, handing her a body board. "Just hang on to this and kick."

Minnie draped her arms over the board, laying her right cheek on its pebbly surface. Feigning effort, she drifted around the pool. As the shadow of the building shifted and the sun warmed her shoulders, languor began to overtake her. She felt her wet-slick thighs rubbing together, their volume allowing them to float easily. Though not necessarily a pretty picture, they reminded her of the manatees. How she missed seeing them rolling companionably below her deck. And how sad that she could never think of them without thinking of Jimmy Simm.

It had been more than a month since the discovery of his body. Nothing more had appeared in the newspaper, and no police had shown up at her door. Still, every night she tossed in her bed, certain that the very next day someone who had seen her at the marina that night would come forward.

While turning her head to place the other cheek on the board, Minnie spotted Catherine James with a client. Catherine probably had been showing the man the activity center, and they now approached the pool. He was tall, square-jawed and barrel-chested, with thinning silver hair. Minnie immediately shoved her legs downward and pushed matted hair from her forehead. Marge Higgins had already slipped from the pool and now sat on its edge, one tanned leg out of the water. She pulled her shoulders back, thrusting her skimpy breasts upward.

"Hi, ladies," Catherine called. "I want you to meet a new resident, Ronald McKay. Mr. McKay is from Denver."

The man removed his sunglasses and gave them a squinty smile. His face was friendly, underlined with jowls. "Nice pool," he said. "These classes open to men?"

Surely he was kidding, Minnie thought, but Marge giggled loudly and said, "Of course. Tuesday and Thursday mornings at eight." Her camera-ready smile spread, as her free leg swished through the water like a pendulum. Minnie thought she might throw up right on the board.

As though to save Mr. McKay embarrassment, Catherine linked her arm in his. "We have a nice barbecue area over here," she said, directing him away.

"Okay, ladies, regroup," Sylvia commanded, clapping her hands for attention. "Let's go back to the shallow end and do some jumping jacks."

Minnie groaned.

She peeled off her bathing suit in the shower and stomped on it to remove the chlorine or whatever they put in pools these days. Every year since the divorce, on the their wedding anniversary date, Antony tried to buy her affections by offering her a trip or some jewelry.

Marlene Baird

"I just can't let this day go by, Min," he always pleaded. "We had thirty-three good years before I made a complete ass of myself. Please, can we remember the happy times?"

She had always refused to acknowledge the date, but this year enough of the pain had bled off. And today he had promised nothing expensive, just a surprise. Minnie rubbed shampoo into her hair. Better than sitting here alone, she thought.

The Cadillac glistened like a giant Christmas tree ornament. Whenever they stopped at a light all eyes turned their way. The older the car got the more attention it attracted, and Minnie was self-conscious about the staring.

"You look especially pretty today," Antony said as if reading her mind. "That copper hair color is fabulous against the rose leather. That's what people are looking at."

"Sure," she chided, but it made her smile. "Where are we going?"

"Since we're almost there, I'll tell you. The manatee sanctuary."

After the divorce, Minnie had sought out distractions where one could go unaccompanied and unnoticed. She'd visited the sanctuary a dozen times. He didn't know that, of course, and thought he was doing something special.

"I wracked my brain to find a destination that was guaranteed to make you smile," Antony said with a hopeful tone. "Make you shake off the Jimmy Simm worries, at least for a few hours."

Minnie And The Manatees

Antony went through the usual complicated parking maneuvers. The car had to be well away from any other vehicles to avoid possible dings, and, today, he was trying to avoid dust and falling tree pollen. It took him five minutes to find the exact spot, which left them a lengthy walk to the entrance. "I should have let you off," he murmured as the sun beat them into the asphalt. He always said that, and Minnie always answered that she'd rather walk. In the humidity her long dress, designed to billow flatteringly, hung straight down, clinging to her legs.

Antony reached to open the entry door, then stopped and pulled her aside to let others pass. "I almost forgot." He pulled a small cardboard box from his pants pocket. Inside was a metal button like those used in political campaigns. About three inches in diameter, it bore the wrinkled face of a manatee and the words, "Save the Gentle Giants." Underneath, in smaller print, it read, "I Helped Protect the Endangered Manatee."

"You are now a member of a manatee protection society. I made a donation in your name."

As he pinned the badge to her dress, just above her heart, she studied his intent face, and a surge of tenderness swept over her. But for that one spectacular mistake, Antony had been a loving and generous husband. It would be so easy to take him in a hug. How she missed having his body close, resting her cheek against his chest. Recognizing that she was entering the danger zone of sentimentality, she forced herself to be honest. He had been unfaithful; she would never lay her cheek against his chest, or anywhere else for that matter. Maybe it was only muscle memory that had been urging her to hug him. She'd heard the term somewhere, probably from Sylvia at the pool.

Lining the interior walls of the building were displays in photographs, graphics and text, telling the story of the West Indian Manatee. Minnie knew a good deal of it by heart and pointed out pertinent facts to Antony.

"They average one thousand pounds in weight, though some in captivity, where they get little exercise, have grown to nearly three thousand."

"That seems cruel," he said.

"The only manatees captured are those who need medical attention, and the only ones kept forever, who get so big, are those unable to fend for themselves. I'll show you one when we go to the tank."

His face fell. "I see, you've been here before."

"A couple of times. But I love it just as much with each visit."

"I should have realized," Antony said.

"They're probably the least aggressive animals on earth. Absolutely harmless. I wonder if that isn't why they have survived, until now. Over millions of years man is the only creature they've inconvenienced."

Minnie And The Manatees

"Well the newly posted speed limits on the waterways are a pain in the neck," Antony answered. "I know people who used to get from their homes to the open water in fifteen minutes. If they obey the slower limits it can take up to forty-five. That cuts into a person's day."

Minnie gave him what she hoped was a withering look. "My heart bleeds."

The huge tank held four manatees. Minnie pointed to the distant back side where a monster floated, resembling a sandy-colored island more than anything alive. Its head seemed the size of a grape on the blubbery body. "Poor thing. She's been here for a long time and will probably never leave. A keeper told me they found her floundering. She had been struck on the head by a boat. They saved her life but she's never recovered her strength. They're afraid she wouldn't survive on her own."

"She doesn't look much like the manatees I see from the boat," Antony said, studying the mound that hunched above the water's surface.

Then that tiny head poked upward and her snout began to twitch in the air. Slowly, the mass sank under the water. Minnie grabbed Antony's arm, pulling him along. "Let's go downstairs."

From the lower level they could see the manatee, swimming underwater, moving toward them. Her bulk became graceful and fluid. She approached the thick glass, then swept upward. They saw sea grasses being spread on the surface, and the water became a swirl of hungry creatures.

"Nothing wrong with her appetite," Antony said, "or mine. How about a burger?"

More relaxed after their lunch, which included a Miller Light, Minnie shifted closer to the Caddy's open window, letting her hair blow. Soft jazz had been playing on the radio and, when the local five o'clock news began, Minnie only half listened until she heard a familiar address, her own. "The woman was found in her condo at the Estero Shores Living complex."

She sat upright and looked at Antony, who turned up the volume. "Do you know a Mrs. Manolo? I can't picture her," he said.

"Did they say Esther Manolo?" Minnie touched her heart. "You met her at least once a long time ago. She was in my bridge group last year. Even at eighty-one she was sharp as anyone."

"Except you." Antony took on a wounded look. "I really think I lost some of my manhood trying to best you in bridge over the years."

"Then it would have better if you'd lost just a little more," Minnie replied flatly. "Poor Esther."

Minnie shook her head as she listened to the reporter finish the story. "Mrs. Manolo's weekly housekeeper found her this morning."

"Did they say how she died?" Minnie asked. "I missed the first part."

"They mentioned that she had emphysema and was on oxygen."

Minnie clicked off the radio. "She came to bridge pulling her portable tank on a buggy with rubber wheels. It never even slowed her down. The only thing she couldn't do very well was carry in groceries, so she would often call Catherine to do that. Catherine would close the office for a few minutes to help Esther."

"The new real estate woman? She doesn't seem the Good Samaritan type."

"Tony, if you could judge women . . . well, I won't finish."

He reached for her hand and held tight as she pretended to pull away. "I should have stayed with my first instinct," he said. "It was dead on."

Antony dropped Minnie off at her condo and drove slowly through quiet residential neighborhoods. If he went home now the evening would be long, but nothing appealed to him except staying with Minnie, and she hadn't invited him in. How many hours had he spent like this, cruising the streets alone, wishing for her company. He congratulated himself that she seemed to have enjoyed the day. At least his purpose, to get her mind off of Jimmy Simm, had been accomplished. But every effort of his to strengthen their relationship seemed puny. Could anything make up for what he had done?

An hour later he drove up to his garage, unaware of how he had arrived there. Low sun poked through the west-facing wall in a dozen places. Antony relished the oily musk which filled the air when he cut the engine. Sitting in the car in the shadowy interior of the garage he thought of Minnie's love for her manatees. Those nurturing instincts had sent her on that early morning mission to disable Simm's boat. It made him wonder what incredible risks she might have taken for her own children. But parenthood had not been in their stars, and Antony thought they had always been complete, just the two of them.

So how did one explain Barbara?

Antony took a deep breath and blew it out. This was not new territory. He had dissected his actions a hundred times, always arriving at the same pathetic conclusion. He was selfish and weak. The only slack he allowed himself was that when he met Barbara he had not been looking.

Fate had a hand, he thought. He almost didn't meet Brian for a beer that evening. Minnie had some late shopping to do and television was hopeless, so he had gone purely out of boredom.

"Antony, I want you to meet my cousin, Barbara Coulter. Barbara, this is Antony Zuccarelli." Brian must have said something like that. Antony could never remember exactly, because, after his first glance at Barbara, his brain had shut down. He could sharply recall short black hair and gold hoop earrings, but not much else about her had registered immediately. His peripheral vision had gone smudgy, his ears buzzed. He wasn't reacting to her appearance

Minnie And The Manatees

alone; the sensation was visceral. Like being knocked off balance by the sneaky aftershock of an earthquake.

The attraction must have been mutual, because they both dropped their eyes at the same time to break the connection. Then, the moment their eyes met again, he felt the need to blink.

He took her offered hand and mumbled, "Glad to meet you."

Antony was vaguely aware of Brian muttering some reason for leaving them and Barbara sliding onto his vacated stool. She sipped straight whiskey, said it felt clean going down. Then she added, "Clean and sharp. Straightens my spine." She sat taller, granting him a smile. There was no confusion about who was in control; he was the only novice involved. Was that part of the attraction—helplessness? Or just part of the excuse.

Antony could think of nothing to say to her that did not sound utterly stupid as he rehearsed it in his head. She finished her drink.

When she rose to leave, he blurted, "How about coffee in the morning?"

She paused, now standing close beside him. "Where?"

Antony arrived at 8:45 and sat in his car. He didn't intend to spy on Barbara; eagerness and nerves had simply brought him early. Soon she arrived in a Chevy sedan. As she swung her legs out of her car he saw they were long and shapely just as he had imagined. He was surprised, however, to realize that she was not beautiful. She was sultry, secretive, behind black sunglasses. And, though dressed in a simple sundress and flat sandals, she walked like a runway model, everything moving at the same time. He tapped on his horn to get her attention and got out of the car.

The sun gods had a cruel side. In the harsh light, fifty some years of intense living were etched on her face. If she thought about it at all, she was not self-conscious. "A lovely morning," she said, taking his arm and smiling.

Antony meant to respond, but as soon as she touched him he lost his voice. Something about this woman's sexuality struck directly to his gut, clouding thought.

When she disengaged herself from him and slid into the leatherette booth, Antony regained some common sense. He held the oversized menu in front of him while he chewed on his tongue. This was insane. Even though he had suggested a restaurant he thought Minnie was unfamiliar with, anyone could walk in. He decided on scrambled eggs with ham, followed by a quick exit. *Nice to meet you. Have a good life.* Then she crossed her legs and the toe of her sandal brushed his calf. He held his breath, hoping she would touch him again.

The waitress came by with the coffee pot and poured two cups.

"Did you know my cousin, Brian, when he played in that awful band?" Barbara asked. Her brown eyes were ageless; they said she had met life full on, that it held no more surprises.

Antony placed the menu off to the side. "I hate that kind of music."

Inane conversation floated amid the aroma of their coffees until there was nothing to say except what was on their minds. And, for that, words were not necessary. They did not order food.

He followed her car through erratic traffic for seven miles, alternately tortured and exhilarated. Her house sat on a neat lawn with a few lanky bushes entwined in a wooden fence. The stucco, blazing white, seemed newly painted. Without waiting for him, she went inside. As he moved down a cool hallway, she called, "This way."

Her bedroom was small and plain. Golden walls, white bedspread and drapes, some decorative pillows, a mirrored closet door. Barbara twisted the rod on the mini-blinds to block the sun, kicked off her sandals and walked toward him.

At first, telling lies to Minnie had curled his insides, diminished him. But after a half dozen times he became almost comfortable with his new, shriveled self. Soon deceit slipped off his tongue easily, and his racing pulse swept guilt aside.

Marlene Baird

Barbara made it so easy, expecting little. And, because they had nothing in common but desire, they were both bored in less than three months. One afternoon they finished the lovemaking, dressed, and moved to the kitchen table. Barbara popped two Cokes and they sat facing one another. She looked old, and he knew he looked common.

"It's been fun, Antony," she said. And his feelings were not even hurt.

Antony slumped forward, draping his arms over the steering wheel, his chin on his chest. To satisfy his lust he had wounded a woman who had never done one thing to hurt him in all their years together. His thoughts turned to the possibility that Minnie might find happiness with someone else and be lost to him forever. Frightened, Antony slid out of the car and secured the garage door. Dust rose over his carefully polished shoes as he walked down the alley. The smell of grilled onions and meat drifted from some open window reminding him of Minnie's Louisiana dirty rice.

Inside his apartment, which faced another building just twenty feet away, it was almost dark. Feet resting on a vinyl ottoman, Antony sat in the gloom and pictured Minnie getting ready for bed. Before stepping into the shower she would check the water temperature, then tuck her hair into that fluffy plastic cap. Did she still hum while lathering herself with bath gel? And the most devastating question: was she always alone?

6

Catherine and Mike often ate at The Bridge, where you could watch quarter-million-dollar yachts tie up after days or perhaps weeks on the water. The motor of a magnificent craft, white with discreet navy trim, had just quieted.

As she ate her orange roughie, Catherine tapped her foot to the rhythm of some mean reggae being played by two musicians with pounding synthesizers. The music was only slighted muted by distance, the men having set up on an outside patio below the main dining room.

Catherine was waiting for the right moment to share her good news about selling Jimmy Simm's condo, but Mike had been moody since he picked her up. He often looked like a big kid, she thought, but tonight he looked like a kid who'd had his bike stolen. Realizing there would be no ideal time, she leaned across the table and whispered eagerly, "The deal closed today. I made almost twelve thousand dollars."

Marlene Baird

"That's all?" he said, disappointment spreading over his face.

"Shoot, Mike. That's a ton of money for me. All I have to do is sit in the office and wait for people to come in. It's not like other real estate jobs where you have to go out and find listings and place advertisements and keep clients happy. I think it's fabulous."

"But, since you won't let me help, you'd need a lot more before you could move." Then his face took on the first animation of the evening. "I saw a terrific place advertised in Naples."

"You forget. Naples is where *you* live. Fort Myers is where I work. But, I promise I'll put this money in the bank until I can add to it. All I want right now is a new dishwasher and a couple of suits for work."

"And shoes," he teased.

"Well, that goes without saying."

A loud crash drew their eyes outside to the white and navy boat. A barefoot woman, her best bikini days behind her, was staring at the deck of her yacht where she'd apparently just dropped something large made of glass. An eight-foot circle of shards sparkled in the lights from the marina and the restaurant. A man appeared from below deck, motioning her not to move. He swept a path to the galley steps so she could walk without being cut. Soon she reappeared in topsiders and a vacuum cleaner and they removed the mess.

"Why would anyone take glass on a boat?" Catherine asked.

"The kitchen in that thing is probably bigger than yours. They don't make many allowances for being on the water." He drained the last of his Jack Daniels, then reached for her hand. His brown eyes went soft as his eyebrows rose in anticipation. "We could charter a boat like that and go away for a few weeks."

"First, I couldn't get off work that long. Second, you wouldn't leave Adrian for more than a few days."

"You're right." Again like a kid, Mike sank back in his chair.

Catherine smiled gently at him. "Let's have coffee and sit for a while." He waved at the waiter in his usual take-command manner, but with melancholy in his eyes. Catherine knew Mike was coming to the realization that no amount of effort, or wishing, would change his son's future, or theirs.

Hoping to get his mind on something else, she asked, "Was that last trip to Atlanta successful?"

He hunched his shoulders then let them drop. "Sure. Made the deal. Real successful."

And that is all the information she would get. He was a manufacturer's representative. Though he was sketchy on details, saying his job bored him and he refused to think about it when it wasn't necessary, she knew he covered a wide territory selling a line of custom cabinetry to building contractors. She'd seen a couple of brochures; they were expensive cupboards with fancy knobs and drawer pulls. At the beginning of their relationship she had pressed him for details about his job and his life, but the more she asked, the more withdrawn he became. Her own parents had been neglectful, instilling in her a crushing need for comfort. So when Mike pulled away she feared abandonment and would capitulate, glossing things over. For a time she even accepted his refusal to discuss marriage.

But one night, during a full-blown argument, Mike finally said that he was already married, swearing that he had no feelings for the woman. His admission didn't truly surprise Catherine. What surprised her was the bitter anger which boiled inside at hearing her suspicion confirmed. She recalled her voice sounding like a shrew as she screamed at him. "So why do you stay with her? I know you're always after money. Is that it? Has she got money?"

She would never forget the anguish and confusion the question caused him. His eyes clouded. His head moved side to side. His mouth opened and closed a couple of times as if he couldn't find the right words. Every ounce of anger had drained from him by the time he looked into her eyes. "How can you say that, Cat. How can you? Don't you know me at all?"

And the story of Adrian had come out.

She remembered how slowly he spoke. It had been a shock, learning that he was to be a father. Parenting had not been in his plans, and at first he was not especially eager. But within a few months he found himself picking up teddy bears and squeeze toys. As he pictured a youngster looking to him for love and guidance, he began to wish for a chance to do better.

"What do you mean, better?" Catherine had asked.

"I'm doing okay, Cat. But I'm a smart enough guy who made some stupid choices. No one in my family ever went to college. Hell, we never even talked about it. I've never set foot in an art museum or attended a play. In the coming baby I could see an opportunity to change that direction, to be part of something larger than myself."

His voice dropped to almost a whisper. "But I hadn't been picturing a baby that looked like Adrian. His little face was flattened, and his fat tongue poked out of a tiny mouth. His eyes slanted upward toward misshapen ears."

Catherine remembered tears sliding down Mike's face as he finished the story. "The first thing I did was touch the bridge of his nose, and his lips curled up at one side. I thought it was a smile." He stopped for a moment. "And, you know what's amazing? I've since learned that that is really all I need from him, a smile."

"Mike, I'm so sorry. It was awful of me to say that about the money. How did his mother handle Adrian's problem?"

Mike's body went stiff. He rubbed his forehead and, again, his words were slow to come, as if each one stabbed him. "She never bonded with Adrian. It was such a shock, she turned away."

The waiter refilled their coffee cups, but Mike pushed his away, letting his fingers rest on the edge of the saucer. Heavy eyes met hers. "At school yesterday, a kid called Adrian a retard."

Catherine reached for his hand. As they waited for the check, she stroked his arm. His heavy jaw worked back and forth against exposing his misery to the world, and Catherine felt even more bound to a man she barely knew.

7

"No, Antony," Minnie said. "Surely you can understand that I don't want you at the funeral where people can see us together. You don't even remember Esther, and it will cause all kinds of speculation."

Disappointment withered his voice, causing Minnie a stab of guilt. "Yeah, I guess. Well, call me afterward?"

"Sure."

Minnie replaced the receiver, frustrated with him. The day at the manatee sanctuary had been lovely, but his attentiveness and kindness had sent her into an emotional tailspin. It seemed like Antony loved her now more than ever. Tears threatened and she slapped her hand on the kitchen counter to stop them. Why had he allowed that woman to come between them? And what a mean twist of fate that now neither of them could be happy.

She blew her nose heartily at the same time the doorbell chimed.

Minnie peered through the fish-eye. A young man, maybe thirty-five, wearing a bulky cotton jacket and jeans, stood on her welcome mat. She watched him for a few seconds as he gazed up and down the cement landing. Just as he reached up as if to knock, she opened the door a crack, leaving the chain in place.

"Mrs. Zuccarelli?" he began, "I'm Detective Wilkins, Fort Myers police. I wonder if you could spare me a few minutes?"

Minnie stared into his eyes while her knees began to tremble. Then they failed her and she doubled over, clutching the door knob to keep from falling.

"Are you all right?" he asked. She heard a thud as the chain reached the end of its length. He was apparently attempting to peer in for a better look.

Minnie took a deep breath, pushed up off her thighs, and stood tall. Here it is, she told herself. She again met his eyes through the four-inch opening of the door. His face had a kindness in it, and calm replaced her fear. It would be a relief to have the suspenseful waiting over with. She would simply tell this young man the truth; that she had disabled Jimmy Simm's boat to keep him from racing down the waterway, with no intent to harm him. Might that make her guilty of negligent homicide or reckless endangerment? Both terms sounded official, though she was unclear of their exact meanings. Might one of them put her in jail for a while? She even felt

Minnie And The Manatees

a hint of curiosity. Would incarceration be the heart-stopping experience she had lived in so many nightmares?

"Do you have some identification?" she asked, because she knew that was how it was done.

He flipped open a leather case, just like on television. "May I come in?"

She unhitched the chain and stepped back. Leading him into the living room, she paused. Anticipating an arrest, she was already lonesome for her well-used furniture which looked lovely now, etched by afternoon sun. She knew she would even miss the dust motes which swam lazily in the air. Scattered magazines, slippers on the footstool, her bedroom pillow on the sofa, told of her long, restless night and exhausted morning. Well, at least there would be no more of that. She saw herself in jailhouse stripes, hoping they were vertical, not horizontal. Her hair would grow long and gray.

She motioned the young man toward the love seat.

"What can I help you with?" she asked, proud of the firmness in her voice.

"Won't you sit down?"

"No." Minnie glanced out her patio doors, her eyes softening as she admired the sparkle on the distant water.

"We're making some routine inquiries about Mrs. Manolo. I understand you were friends."

She blinked, turning to face the detective. "Esther?"

She took three hesitant steps and sat heavily on the low footstool, almost falling. Not Jimmy Simm, she thought, not Jimmy Simm. Relief drained all Minnie's bravado, and her legs felt like the wiggly noodles at the pool.

"Why would you be making inquiries about Esther?"

"It's only to complete the paperwork. Did you happen to see her in the days before her death?"

"I haven't seen Esther for several weeks. I stopped playing bridge some time ago. She has closer neighbors than me." Minnie pressed her hand over a nerve that was jumping in her thigh.

"I'm sorry to make you so nervous," he said. "We're talking with everyone. However, all of you who live in this building can see her entry door and you have an especially clear view, straight across the waterway. Did you see anything or anyone the evening before she died, or, perhaps early in the morning?"

"I'm out on my deck every morning before dawn. Nothing then, for sure. I don't know about the evening. Won't you tell me why you're investigating? After all, she was quite ill."

"Her breathing tube was not attached to the oxygen tank, and her door had not been locked. Possibly she merely forgot to lock the door, and

Minnie And The Manatees

perhaps, in her sleep, she accidentally became detached from the oxygen."

"That's a lot of conjecture, but I can't imagine anyone doing her harm."

The detective took a card from his pocket, put it on the coffee table, and rose. "Will you call me if anything comes to mind?"

As soon as he left, the nerve in Minnie's leg stopped contracting. She stretched out on the sofa. Her head sank into the pillow, and slept like a cat in the sun for three and a half hours.

The next day Minnie stood at Esther's grave site, a warm drizzle dripping from her umbrella. About fifty people had attended the church service, but fewer traveled to the cemetery for the burial. She had met Esther's daughter, Joan, but no one else in the family. "My mom was happy living down here," Joan said to her. "She often mentioned how nice her neighbors were, and your name came up more than once." There was no indication in her voice that she had any suspicions about the cause of her mother's death.

After the burial, as people dispersed, Joan moved alongside Minnie. "We need to sell the condo as soon as possible. Is there someone you would recommend as an agent?"

It was then Minnie realized that Catherine, probably Esther's most constant visitor, had not been at the service.

Minnie listened to the phone ring several times in the sales office before Catherine answered. "Estero Shores," she said.

"Catherine, its Minnie Zuccarelli. We missed you at Esther's funeral."

"Just a second, Minnie." There was a click followed by a hollow hum, as if she'd been put on hold.

Minnie was about to hang up when Catherine finally returned. "Sorry, I was with some interested clients. I am sorry about this afternoon. Esther was a dear, but I simply couldn't lock up the office for that long. There's no one to cover for me."

"You'd think the management would make some arrangements. What if you're sick some day?"

"Touch wood, I'm never sick. How was the service?"

Minnie gave her a few details, then mentioned that Esther's daughter would be selling the condo. "Would you like her number? She'll be staying in town for a few days."

"Sure, thanks," Catherine answered. "Minnie, I heard there has been a detective nosing around. Did he talk to you?"

"Yes, but I can't believe anyone would have harmed Esther."

"Me neither, yet it is a little spooky. You're alone. . . you always lock your door don't you?"

"Gosh, Catherine, you gave me a chill. Don't think that way."

As Minnie repeated Joan's phone number to Catherine, she glanced at her doorway, noting that she'd neglected to throw the bolt.

"Oh, and Minnie," Catherine said, "I've decided to try those acrylic nails. Do you take evening appointments?"

Minnie had been hunched over her manicure table for most of the day, and all the muscles in her back and shoulders were crying for relief. But she had let her cupboards get bare and needed to shop for groceries in spite of being tired. She was leaning over the display of green beans, trying to decide if they were fresh, when the overhead sprayer suddenly came on. Waiting, she pulled herself upright, and kneaded the small of her back with both hands. The stretch felt so good she didn't even care that she was in public. She pushed her elbows severely behind her and leaned even further back. Looking up, she was surprised to see folded lawn chairs stacked on a shelf above the produce section.

A voice, speaking her name with a question mark at the end, made her turn.

"Ah, I thought it was you," Ronald McKay said. "A tough day?"

Minnie realized her breasts were pointing at his collarbone. She dropped her hands to her side, feeling heat in her cheeks.

"Haven't seen you at the pool," he said. "I hope having a man attend the class hasn't scared you off."

Minnie attempted a small laugh. "Of course not," she said, though that was exactly what had happened. She missed many classes because it had become much too difficult to time her arrival before him, and her departure after him, so as not to have to climb in and out of the water with his eyes on her. She often felt that they were.

"I've been too busy. Did you buy that boat you were talking about?"

"I settled on a smaller one, something easier to handle. I'd love to take you out on the water some day." His gaze was too direct and, though he was talking about an innocent trip, he seemed to be saying much more.

"Thanks, but I'm not a deep water person."

"Well then, how about a cup of coffee after we finish shopping?"

"Actually," Minnie said, pointing, "I've got ice cream."

Ronald McKay picked up her Pecan Swirl and settled it among his Chocolate Crunch and frozen foods, which resided in a small cooler in his buggy. "This thing is magic; it will keep."

Minnie felt so flustered and heated at his insistence that she wanted to grab one of his bags of frozen vegetables and hold it up to her forehead. There seemed no decent way to escape.

Minnie And The Manatees

The supermarket occupied the center spot in a strip mall of eleven businesses, one of which was the shop where Minnie worked. The mall also included a small coffee shop, so, after depositing their groceries in their cars, Minnie and Ronald entered the cafe.

"Hi, Minnie," the waitress, Sally, called. "I'll be right with you." Her eyebrows rose as Ronald put his hand on Minnie's waist and guided her to a booth.

"Just coffees," Minnie said.

"I guess lots of people know you around here," Ronald said, sitting across from her. He had some trouble fitting into the narrow space between the table and the bench. He enjoys his ice cream as much as I do, Minnie thought.

Sally arrived with the coffees and the same astounded look on her face. Minnie shook her head slightly when their eyes met, and Sally went away unsatisfied.

"I'm in here a lot. The shop where I work is just a few doors down. I'm a manicurist."

"Ah, that accounts for your beautiful nails. I always admire them."

Where was he from? Wasn't it Denver? Did living at a high altitude affect people strangely? Here sat a man who did water exercises with women, shopped with a cooler, and studied women's fingernails. Was he gay? One way to find out.

"Were you ever married?" she asked, casually sipping her coffee.

Ronald chuckled, then leaned toward her and smiled into her eyes. "Getting down to the nitty-gritty? I'm flattered. No, I've never been married."

Did you live with your mother? she wanted to ask.

"And I didn't live with my mother," he said.

Minnie spit coffee half way across the table before she could get her napkin in place. It dribbled out her nose while she coughed uncontrollably.

Ronald, always so composed, jumped back from the onslaught. He raised his crisp, white shirt sleeves out of the way. Then he stood, wiggling the table as he tried to get up. He patted her back, clearly unsure about whether or not to pound on it.

She held up her hand to stop him. "I'm okay."

Then Sally appeared, concern on her face.

"Really. Please." Minnie waved them both back. She cleared her throat, dried her eyes, and buried the stained napkin under her right thigh.

"It went down the wrong pipe," Ronald offered.

"Apparently," Minnie croaked, her throat still tight.

She couldn't look him in the face. "I think we'd better get that ice cream into our freezers."

While Ronald retrieved her ice cream from his car, Minnie was grateful for the cooling night air on her face which burned from embarrassment. What a bungled meeting, she thought. He must think me an idiot.

"Enjoy," he said, handing her the Pecan Swirl. "We'll try coffee again another time, okay?"

"I promise not to spit it on you."

He chuckled, then waved as she pulled away.

The underground garage was always a little unnerving at night. Pools of harsh light made the shaded parts seem even spookier. Luckily, there was a rolling cart available near the elevator shaft and Minnie transferred her groceries quickly onto its two deep shelves. Once inside the bright elevator she felt relieved. Seeing that ridiculous scene in her mind's eye—her shock at Ronald's words about not living with his mother and his discomfort when she choked—made a giggle form in her chest. By the time she reached the sixth floor and opened her door she was laughing at herself and at him.

She grabbed the ringing phone.

"Hello."

"You sound happy," Antony said.

"Just thinking of something funny."

"Can you share?" he asked.

"You had to be there."

"It's getting late. I was beginning to worry."

"I stopped for coffee with a friend."

"Oh." The pause told Minnie he wanted to ask more, and it was the first time Antony's protectiveness had seemed intrusive. Usually she was glad to have him keeping an eye out for her at night.

"What were you up to today?" she asked, tucking the softened ice cream into the freezer one-handed.

"Had the car detailed. Ate a burger for dinner. Watched TV. Nothing special." His voice dropped a notch when he added, "Missed you."

"Antony—"

"Sorry. Not your problem. Try to get a good sleep tonight."

"You, too," she replied.

By the time she returned the cart to the parking garage the coffee spitting episode did not seem so funny. It had been disingenuous of her to assume Ronald was gay. He was a very nice man, and she hoped she hadn't ruined her chances.

8

When Catherine opened the door to the beauty shop and stepped inside, the air almost stopped her. It was so thick with hair spray, bleaching fumes and manicure chemicals that she didn't want to breathe. Six hairstyling stations ran down the right side of the long, narrow room. Four were sparkling clean, ready for tomorrow, with only two occupied this late in the day. One stylist had just finished a man's haircut and was shaking hair from his protective cape. In the other chair sat an older woman with as little hair as a newborn.

Down the left side of the room were the manicure cubicles, divided by half walls. Catherine found Minnie in the third one, her thighs rolling over the edge of a narrow chair. Minnie has such a pretty face, she thought, it's a shame she has let herself get so heavy.

"Gosh, how can you breathe in here?" Catherine asked, depositing her purse on the floor and sitting in the chair across Minnie's small table.

Minnie looked up as she folded a clean, white towel and slid it into position, expertly smoothing it with her hand. "Hi Catherine. It gets bad by evening, but I guess we're all immune by now." Minnie pulled her shoulders back and swiveled her head, stretching her neck.

"Long day?" Catherine asked.

"Seven clients. That's just about enough at my age." Minnie took Catherine's hands in her own and studied her nails. "You want the nails any longer?"

"You can do that?"

"Sure."

"Maybe just a bit then, but nothing too exotic. Like yours would be nice, but I don't know about the yellow color."

"You mean Copper Mystery," Minnie said, grinning at her. "A lot of gals your age like the French nails."

Catherine raised her eyebrows.

"They have a natural finish, with white tips."

"Oh, I've seen those. No, I'd like some color."

Minnie handled Catherine's fingers, one by one, for a half hour. She shaped each nail with a file, dusted them, and applied the extensions. Then she added the acrylic, which dried immediately, and filed again. Minnie's hands were warm, her touch soothing. Catherine felt the day's tension draining away; if she'd allowed it, her head might have lolled forward. But it was more than relaxation—there was an intimacy in the contact which she found calming. "You have healing hands," she said.

Minnie looked up sharply, blinking. "Healing?"

"Yes. I guess it's similar to a massage, though I've never had one."

"I read once that often the masseuse receives energy back from the person they are working on. That's a nice thought. Send me some good vibes." Minnie had dabbed some oil on each cuticle and, using her thumbs, rubbed it energetically into the skin all around Catherine's new, elegant nails.

"Have you decided on a color?" she asked.

Bottles of polish rose in tiers on either side of Minnie's table, numbering maybe three dozen in all. Catherine was curious about some of the silvers and the purple-blues, but chose a rosy tone.

"That will be terrific, especially with that pink suit," Minnie said, shaking the bottle. "First, go to the restroom at the back and scrub that oil off your nails and dry them well."

As Catherine moved toward the restroom, she caught Minnie pulling her shoulders back again, stretching. Catherine had noticed the fatigue in her face, and adjusted her opinion of Minnie. Sitting still all day would make anyone put on weight, and she hoped she would not have to work so hard when she was Minnie's age. She washed her longer, perfectly-shaped nails and looked at them with admiration; Minnie was a craftsman, and an artist.

"This color is great on you," Minnie said, applying the first coat of Brazen Blush. "A lot of gals can't wear something with this much blue in it because it makes their skin look yellow."

"How long have you been doing this, Minnie?"

"Four years. I used to be a bank teller. But I like both jobs because of the public contact. Nothing's more interesting than people."

"Real estate is that way, too. Say, didn't I see you yesterday walking along the waterway with our newest resident, Ronald McKay?" Catherine was surprised to see Minnie's cheeks redden.

"He's a nice man," Minnie said, keeping her eyes directed to her work. Catherine knew Minnie was divorced, and had always simply thought of her as being alone. Now, she wondered whether Minnie dated, whether she had children or other family nearby. But she was not about to find out, as Minnie changed the subject.

"Have you anyone interested in Esther's place?" Minnie asked, picking up the bottle of clear top coat.

"Two buyers are looking at it. A Jewish couple from New Jersey, in their seventies I'd say, and a local, younger couple who apparently won some minor lottery."

Minnie And The Manatees

Minnie stopped in mid-stroke, her eyes going distant. "Wouldn't that be fun? I don't even need millions. A few hundred thousand would be nice. Just to give me a pillow."

The thought of Minnie needing a pillow almost brought tears. Catherine thought of the financial security Mike offered her, the opportunities youth itself laid out before her, the advantage beauty carried with it.

"Are you dating, Minnie?"

Minnie's eyes met hers. Catherine thought she could see stories wanting to be told but Minnie simply shook her head. "All done," she announced. "What do you think?"

Catherine looked at her hands. She'd never thought them particularly attractive, but the perfect ovals made her fingers look longer, and her skin glowed from the massage. She told Minnie she'd done a fabulous job, and thought of the bits of pleasure Minnie brought to women every day with her talent and her tender hands. Selling real estate seemed crass in comparison.

As Minnie put her equipment back into shallow drawers she said, "You can sit here a minute and let them dry." She tossed the towel into a laundry bin, sprayed her Formica counter top with something that smelled good, and wiped it until it shone.

When Minnie finished with her, Catherine experienced a stab of loneliness. "Do you have plans for dinner?" she asked.

Minnie was clearly surprised at the invitation. After a moment she said, "I was just now trying to get interested in the leftover meat loaf in my fridge."

"How about Chinese? There's a little place a few blocks away that I just love."

Minnie followed Catherine into the restaurant, feeling blubbery. The straight cut of Catherine's skirt hugged her narrow hips. Her spiked heels clicked flirtatiously, while Minnie's work shoes made a squeegee sound. Solitary meat loaf seemed a better idea.

It was the sister to a million other American-Chinese restaurants. Delicate bird and flower paintings, lots of gold and red, mild-mannered, capable servers, and a wonderful aroma. They were led to a round table and served tea. "Have to have sweet and sour pork," Catherine said, opening her menu. "Can't do without that. What's your favorite?"

Minnie had to think. Antony's favorite came to mind—cashew chicken. He could eat two full servings of it. "Fried rice with shrimp, I guess," she said.

Once they discussed possible dishes to share, and had finally ordered, the only thing they had in common was the tea. Both sipped at the tiny cups, smiling. Minnie wished she had asked for a glass of wine. Her ears began to burn from the silence.

Minnie And The Manatees

"Excuse me, Catherine, but I have to say I imagined you having a dinner date every night of the week. You must have men calling you constantly."

"Oh, I have a special friend. He's the only person I date."

"Does he ever come to your office? Might I have seen him around the property?"

"Mike is out of town a lot, and when he is home he's pretty busy." Catherine pulled a tissue out of her purse and blew her nose. "Allergies," she was quick to point out, but Minnie knew better. These were sudden tears, apparently brought on by the mention of Mike.

"Want to talk about it?"

Catherine dabbed at her eyes and glanced around. There was only one other table occupied. "No. Not really." She closed her eyes against more tears.

Minnie took her hand, rubbing it gently with her thumb. "It can't be that bad."

Catherine withdrew her hand and seemed to gather herself. "I had the oddest message on my answering machine last night. Mike said he would be out of touch for a while, maybe quite a while. As I said, he often goes away on business, but he always calls. He left no phone number, nothing."

"Oh, gosh, that could be anything," Minnie said quickly, though nothing came to mind.

"I wouldn't worry so much if it was only for myself, but he has a young son who's not well.

Mike's never left him for more than a couple of days."

"Where's the boy's mother?"

Catherine sat perfectly still, like she'd been flash-frozen, her model's face sculpted in shock. Then she bit her bottom lip. "Oh, God. That's it. Why didn't I see it?"

"See what?"

"He's gone back to her."

"His ex-wife?"

Catherine hesitated, looking into Minnie's eyes. "They aren't actually divorced. Does that shock you?"

"I've been on the other end of that situation, Catherine. My viewpoint is tainted."

"Maybe I've been an idiot all along," Catherine said.

"I felt that way, too, at first."

"When?"

"When my husband cheated on me."

"Minnie, I'm sorry to bring this up."

"It's okay. I felt stupid at first, too. Like an old dog who'd been happily curled asleep on the carpet while the world carried on around me. It was such a shock, I couldn't connect with anything or anyone. Even the women in the bank, who I'd worked with for years, seemed to have some insight that I lacked."

"But you've come around," Catherine said. "You seem fine."

"Most days are pretty good." She patted Catherine's hand. "Remember you don't know what's really happening."

The steaming pile of shrimp fried rice was barely dented and Catherine's sweet and sour pork left almost untouched, when they paid their bill. In the parking lot Catherine began to cry again, and Minnie hugged her. "You might have it all wrong," she murmured, hoping. She remembered how Antony's deception had stripped her bare and left her bleeding. Even though Catherine might be the other woman, she wished that pain on no one. "Will you be okay to drive? I could give you a lift."

"I can manage, but thanks. And thanks for listening, Minnie."

When Minnie got home, after nine o'clock, there were two messages from Antony. Catherine's confessions had brought his affair freshly to the surface, and she didn't particularly want to talk to him. But when he called again, she told him about the visit from Detective Wilkins.

"I was sick to death of course to see him at my door, but now I almost wish he *had* come to talk about Jimmy Simm. It might be best to just get it over with."

"Don't be hasty, Min."

"No. Of course, what I need to do is put it out of my mind. God, how I wish I had minded my own business."

"You did a gallant thing," Antony said, but then he would say anything to try to make her feel better.

9

Four days later Catherine heard Mike's car pull up in front of her house, followed by the dying of the engine. The card accompanying yesterday's rainbow bouquet of tiger lilies had promised this seven o'clock visit, and he was right on time. She checked herself in the hall mirror again, noting that her eyes still looked old and drawn from days and nights of worry.

His key poked at the lock and she heard him cursing as he twisted it back and forth. Then he pounded on the door. "Cat? It's me. My damn key won't work."

She released the dead bolt and opened the door a crack. "That's because I changed the lock."

Mike's eyebrows drew together and his mouth dropped open. "What?"

"The first of many changes in my life," she said.

"Oh, Cat, let me in. This is silly."

"Five days and nights with no word from you. No explanation. That was cruel, Mike."

He pushed gently on the door, but she held her place.

She saw him glance left and right as if worried the neighbors might be interested in their conversation, then he lowered his voice. "It was bad of me, Cat, but I had no choice. You have to let me explain." He put one hand high on the door frame, leaning toward her. Perspiration darkened his shirt under the arm and Catherine saw a sheen of it forming on his flushed cheeks. His eyes begged her to let him in.

She allowed the door to swing open, and his face changed to that of a man who had just been granted a reprieve from the gallows. He didn't come inside, but waited for her invitation.

As she stepped out to the landing and wrapped her arms around him, Mike's upper body shook, and he sighed. He lifted her and carried her inside, kicking the door shut. His face was buried in her neck and she felt hot tears. "Don't ever do that again, please," he whispered.

After their lovemaking she saw that he was fighting more tears. Catherine cradled his head. "What can be that bad?" she asked. "Is it Adrian?"

He shifted away from her, sitting upright, brushing at his face with his forearm. "I have to tell you something that might drive you away, and that would kill me."

Catherine reached out to stroke his face. "Nothing could do that. I've just been angry and frightened; I never stopped loving you. Not for an instant."

"Let's get dressed," he said, "then talk."

Giving Mike some privacy to gather himself, Catherine put on a terry-cloth robe and turned on the two lamps in the living room. Tucking herself into a corner of the brown tweed sofa, she looked around the room at her inheritance—the mismatched furniture and cheap rugs. She knew she should get rid of all the junk, but this house and its contents were all she had of her parents. They had both been salespeople, her dad pushing cars and her mom promising beauty through expensive skin treatments. But both had played as hard as they worked with no thought for the future. Catherine did not regret their poor financial planning, they didn't owe her that. What they owed her was love and attention. She saw herself, an eleven-year old girl, coming home from school to an empty house. That pattern remained for years afterwards. Except for her small frame, the house would be empty and hollow until well after midnight. There were countless days like that, but how long could you blame people for being simply what they were?

She wrapped her arms around herself against a sick chill that was stealing through her body, and turned her thoughts away from the past. Mike was so upset tonight that she feared the worst. If what he had to tell her was something that would force them to part, she would be alone again.

When Mike entered the room he looked ten years older than usual. She patted the cushion beside her and he sat. He took one of her hands and she felt skin as cold as her own. "Cat, when I was young, sixteen, seventeen, I was a punk hood." He stared into her eyes but she didn't allow any emotion to show there. "I stole cars for joy rides, shoplifted. Went to juvenile detention a couple of times. I knew better. I don't even remember what the hell I was rebelling against. Maybe it was boredom."

"That was a long time ago."

"Yes, and no." He squeezed her hand, holding tight. "In high school Janice and a couple of her friends hung with us guys, but managed to stay out of trouble with the police. We all experimented with drugs a bit, but I never knew she got hooked. I only learned about it years later."

Mike had mentioned Janice's name only twice before, in connection with Adrian's doctor appointments. Every time Catherine heard the name she experienced a fresh sadness. This time it was tinged with pity. "And she's still using drugs?"

"She's been in and out of treatment. Sometimes clean for a couple of years at a time."

"Did that have something to do with Adrian's problems?"

"What do you mean?"

"I mean, did her drug problem affect the baby?"

"No," he said. "Not at all. It's not caused by anything like that. It's a chromosome imbalance."

"So, is that where you've been these past few days, holding her hand?"

He shook his head and dropped his gaze to the carpet. "I saw some grease-ball supplier parked on our street. He was sitting in his car waiting for me to leave the house so he could visit her. I lost it. I hauled him out of his seat and beat the shit out of him. It was bad, Cat. I've been in jail."

Even though Catherine had braced herself, this blindsided her. The raw ferocity of the act was frightening, and she also suffered the knowledge that Mike was putting himself in danger to protect Janice. Of course he would, but she saw herself shoved aside just a bit more.

Mike turned his whole body toward her. "Cat, I feel like I'm going to crack in two. I'm not the kind of man you deserve. My life is so friggin' complicated. You should have someone who can be with you always, spend every minute with you. And I can't see an end to my situation."

Catherine fingered the sash of her robe and thought a long time before speaking. "If Janice has such problems, couldn't you get full custody of Adrian?"

He shook his head. "I couldn't possibly separate them, Cat. He loves her to distraction.

He sees only good in everybody. And she's never harmed him."

"Are you sure?"

"I worried a lot when he was younger, and kept a sharp eye. But he's been old enough to tell me for many years, and there's never been even a suggestion. Besides, I have to work. I'd have to leave him with someone else all day, sometimes overnight."

Catherine thought, what about me? I could help. But somehow she never fit into Mike's plans and knew it would be useless to make any further suggestions.

"Do you have to work so hard? All those hours?"

"Adrian will never be able to care for himself. In case something happens to me, I need to leave him well provided for."

Catherine took Mike's hand in both of hers. Whatever his situation, everything condensed into his love for his son. "Is that all you have to tell me?"

He nodded.

"It's a sad story, but I haven't heard anything that makes me love you less."

Long after midnight Catherine sat upright in her magnificent bed. She had been honest with Mike, she didn't love him less. But it was clearer than ever that she was investing all of herself in an unpredictable, probably unhappy, future. And now she had questions which frightened her. How

Minnie And The Manatees

likely was it that this incident of brutality was an isolated one? Mike was thirty years removed from those teenage crimes. Had he been a model citizen all that time, until just now? And, had he not landed in jail, she would never have known about it. She lay awake for hours wondering what else he had not told her.

Marlene Baird

10

At three o'clock on a Thursday afternoon, Minnie felt wonderfully decadent, sitting with Ronald McKay in the open-air bar on Fort Myers beach, sipping her second rum and Coke. Above the noise of a young man belting out quasi-Jimmy Buffett music, she could hear shouts of small children chasing one another at the water's edge.

Minnie guessed this would be considered their first date. You could hardly count the evening she poked her boobs at him in the grocery store, then spit coffee at him later. And last week's walk along the condo waterways, though it had stretched into quite a lengthy one, had actually begun as an accidental meeting.

Ronald gazed intently seaward, so she stole a look at him. He was a big man, which made her feel more delicate than when she was with Antony. Antony was so lithe and quick-moving that she felt ponderous beside him. Not that she'd been next to Antony lately; he still called every day, but somehow they hadn't managed to get together.

Earlier, as she and Ronald walked the long white beach with pant legs rolled, Minnie had enjoyed watching a family of five youngsters from about two to ten years old devouring huge ice cream cones. They melted too fast, creating sticky messes on chins and fingers, but their mother was well-prepared with a hand towel which she regularly dipped into the gulf. Minnie wondered whether things would have ended differently if she and Antony had been blessed with children. Would he have acted as he did if a child were also involved? Then she chided herself. At the time of the divorce any child of theirs would have been grown, not an endearing little sweetheart gripping Daddy's fingers, holding him back.

"Oh, goodness," Ronald said.

Minnie followed his gaze to the end of the long pier, and saw the cause of his concern. A fisherman had snagged a pelican. Huge gray-brown wings flapped anxiously, slapping the surface of the water. From their distance it was impossible to tell exactly where on the bird's body the hook had imbedded itself, though it didn't seem to be on the head or neck.

"Will it be permanently injured?" Ronald asked.

"I doubt it," Minnie said. "They are strong, resilient birds. But getting him free might be a problem."

Marlene Baird

A crowd was gathering behind the fisherman on the pier. From her vantage point, Minnie could see him leaning over the wooden rail. His pole arched, then bent almost double, as he wound in his line. The dripping pelican began to rise from the water and all flapping stopped. As some animals do when in danger, he seemed to freeze.

"Surely that small line can't hold him," Ronald said. "Perhaps the man is hoping it will break and the bird will fall free."

"No. He could cut the line. He must be trying to bring it to the deck."

The awkward bird, hanging sideways, so lanky and disheveled, looked like a strange sea creature rising slowly upward toward the pier. When it was within reach, several men grabbed at wings and feet and lifted it to the railing. Immediately the pelican righted itself and perched there, still making no move to escape. Several hands were involved in locating and then freeing the hook. After a moment the crowd backed away. The pelican took them all in, and apparently deciding no free food was at hand, raised his angled wings and flew off.

A deep grin creased Ronald's face as he turned to Minnie. "Imagine that," he said. "I love Florida." Genuine happiness for the pelican lit his full face, and Minnie smiled at his finding pleasure in something so simple.

Minnie And The Manatees

"We Floridians are a kind lot," she teased. "Generally, we release anything we can't eat, and pelican would be tough."

He winked at her. "And if, once hooked, we don't wish to be released, would someone take us home for dinner?"

During the last few weeks Minnie's mind, when left to wander, had been turning to sexual thoughts. She assumed it was simply because the partner-less years were catching up with her. Now she blushed crimson at what she perceived to be a double entendre in Ronald's perhaps innocent remark. She wondered if these distracting thoughts hadn't started when she met him.

Hoping he would think her blush merely sunburn, she put her glass to her forehead. Should she invite him back for dinner? She moved the cool glass to her cheek as she mentally tallied the items in her pantry. The only fresh meat was some hamburger.

"Do you like Louisiana dirty rice?" she asked. Then, sensing the suggestiveness in the word dirty, she flushed even more.

Ronald grinned broadly. "Two novel experiences in one day. Fabulous."

As they drove back to her place, Minnie ran the dirty rice recipe around in her head, though concentrating was no easy task. Her invigorating walk on the beach, combined with the two drinks and the hot sun, turned her thoughts toward napping. She knew that would be fine with Ronald, were she ready. And she was getting ready. Almost dozing in the plush car seat, she saw the two of them filling her queen-sized bed. She allowed long-ignored sensations to tease her body.

"You going to sleep?" Ronald asked.

"Heavens, no."

"Your eyes were closed."

"They were not," Minnie snapped.

"Okay, they were open." Ronald chuckled. "But you seem dangerously relaxed."

Another suggestive remark? In her hazy condition it was difficult to judge.

As they turned off of Estero Boulevard into the condo complex, an ambulance was leaving the grounds. It moved quickly, but had no lights flashing or siren blaring.

"Looks like a false alarm, thank goodness," Minnie said, thoroughly awake. "Let's stop at the office. Maybe Catherine knows what's happening."

Minnie hadn't been in the sales office for a couple of years. The wall map, clustered with tiny flags and colored pins, had at least doubled in size. When completed, the complex would not resemble the compact community she and Antony had thought they were buying into.

"We saw the ambulance," Minnie said, tapping lightly on Catherine's open office door. "Do you know what happened?"

Catherine looked up from her paperwork and waved them in. Minnie thought she looked harried, and feared her boyfriend had still not called to explain his absence.

"Mr. Broomfield had an accident. He seems fine but they took him in for observation."

"I don't think I know him," Minnie said.

"Building 4. He's been here about two years. He was frail and used a walker. He fell into the waterway just around the corner," she said, pointing through the wall behind her. "He was too weak to climb out onto the slippery bank. Luckily, two other residents heard his cries." Catherine leaned back in her swivel chair. "And we can probably expect another visit from the police."

Minnie plunked down in the visitor's chair. "No. Why?"

"Mr. Broomfield claims he was pushed."

"By whom?" Minnie blurted.

"He said it was from behind and he didn't see the person."

Minnie looked up at Ronald. "Esther Manolo, now this man. Makes me nervous."

While the rice cooled and the meat sizzled, Minnie chopped onion, garlic, celery and green pepper into minute pieces. She was glad to be busy, since her thoughts kept turning to that young detective in the loose cotton jacket. Wilkins was his name. She couldn't imagine how she would be able to respond if he came knocking on her door again. As soon as she began to feel distanced from Jimmy Simm something happened to bring it all back.

"You're not Southern," Ronald called from the living room. "Where did you get this recipe?"

"From a friend. I like it better with some sausage added to the hamburger, but I don't have any today."

"It smells wonderful already."

Minnie heard him put down the newspaper, then he was in the kitchen doorway. "Are you really concerned about your friend's death and that accident today?"

"It might not be an accident. Still, I shouldn't be surprised that we lose residents, with all the elderly people here now."

"The man who owned my place, Simm . . . I didn't get the impression he was old. Wasn't it some kind of boating accident?"

Minnie concentrated on smooth, determined movements to disguise her anxiety. Scooping with both hands, she tossed the mound of chopped vegetables into the browning meat. The sizzle increased as she stirred vigorously. "I don't know if anyone knows for sure what happened to him." She sprinkled salt, pepper and cayenne on the mix.

Ronald came to stand beside her. "That smells so terrific." He put an arm around her shoulder, touching her bare skin. "You're cold," he announced, rubbing her upper arm. "Do you not feel well?"

Minnie And The Manatees

"Just too much outdoors, I think. I'll be fine."

"Let me set the table, then we'll eat and I'll get out of your hair. It's been a busy day." She pointed him to the drawer that held the placemats.

Minnie dumped the cooked rice on top of the meat mixture and combined it thoroughly, scraping up the dark pieces on the bottom of the pan. After scooping the finished product into a serving bowl, she threw a handful of chopped green onions on top.

Bending over to pull a pre-mixed salad from the fridge, she suddenly felt dizzy, as the detective's face drifted before her. She stood with the cellophane bag in her hand and couldn't remember where to find the kitchen scissors. Dazed, she looked at Ronald, sitting at the table, waiting. One of the placemats he'd pulled from the drawer had a coffee stain. The paper napkins were her old wrinkled ones with the gaudy pink flowers. He probably hated fat-free dressing. A giant tear rolled down her right cheek.

Ronald jumped from his chair. "What is it, Minnie?"

She brushed the tear away with the back of her hand. "I haven't the slightest idea. Probably I just need food."

Ronald insisted on helping her clean up, though she'd much rather he had simply left.

Marlene Baird

Finally closing the door behind him, the early afternoon's pleasures seemed years away.

Minnie dialed Antony's number and, following his taped message, said, "I'm scared. Call me."

At two o'clock in the morning she fell asleep on the sofa, still waiting for his call, the phone cradled against her stomach.

11

It was five-thirty the next afternoon before Antony called her at the shop. "I'm sorry. I should have let you know I'd be away. We went on an overnighter down the coast."

Minnie tucked the phone into the crook of her neck and continued shaping her client's nails. "Who's we?"

Antony paused for several seconds, then spoke with a strain in his voice. "Actually, I went with Brian."

The warmth drained from Minnie's fingers and they went stiff. She accidentally dragged the nail file across Mrs. Gertz's bare skin, causing the woman to jerk her hand away. Brian, the friend who had introduced Antony to Barbara. Just hearing the name could still do this to her. Minnie smiled an apology and took Mrs. Gertz's hand again. When would she be able to move through her days in confidence without being tripped up by one or two syllables.

Antony could have lied to her, and she almost wished he had. To be mean, to remind him of her pain, she almost asked if Barbara had been a part of the trip even though she knew the answer. Minnie never doubted Antony's claim that the affair had been short-lived. From the moment she learned of Barbara's existence to this day, Antony had done nothing but try to reassure her of his love.

"Min, are you there?" Antony said.

"Yes."

"It wasn't a good idea. Too much beer and not enough fishing. You know Brian."

"And so do you."

"Yeah, well, I've been feeling at loose ends the last couple of weeks. But I shouldn't be bothering you with that. Why did you call and say you were scared?"

"I can't talk about it right now." Minnie's legs ached and it seemed impossible to draw her shoulders back squarely. Mrs. Gertz tipped her head, as if trying to get a better look at Minnie's face.

"Something is really troubling you," Antony said. "Please, let's talk."

"This is my last client."

"I'll pick you up in half an hour."

Antony had bought two chicken dinners, which filled the car with an aroma that made Minnie's mouth water. He drove to a small park, tucked into the end of a residential cul-de-sac

Minnie And The Manatees

where they had a view of the gulf and the sunset. While he spread a red and black checked blanket just where the grass met the beach, Minnie retrieved the food and a bottle in a brown bag.

"Forgot glasses," Antony said, slapping his forehead with the palm of his hand.

"We can swig," Minnie said.

She sat on the lower edge of the blanket so she could dig her toes into the sand, then pulled the bottle from its bag. "You brought champagne?"

"I wanted to make it special."

"Well, we can't swig this, it will have to wait for another time. Just as well, since I'm in no mood for a celebration."

Antony unfolded the cardboard boxes, speaking hesitantly. "My going off with Brian . . . that didn't upset you, did it? Because there is no reason it should."

"No reason?"

"Now, I mean."

"You can do what you want, Tony." She knew he hated her calling him Tony.

He shifted on the blanket, making her look directly at him. "Don't do that, please. Don't put more distance between us."

"What do you mean, more distance?"

"Minnie, you've sounded different on the phone lately. We don't talk as long. I feel like you're not confiding in me." Minnie opened her mouth to object, but he stopped her with a gesture of his hand. "I'm not saying I deserve such confidences, just that there has been a subtle change recently." He touched his chest. "I feel it here, and it makes me panic."

Minnie looked out at the graying water and wondered if Ronald McKay would become a big enough part of her life that she should mention him.

Antony touched her shoulder. "Min, I can barely bring myself to ask, but are you seeing someone?"

For the first time since the early craziness of the divorce, Minnie acted with deliberate cruelty. She kept her gaze on the water and said nothing. Sensing his anxiety, so easily created, sent a rush of power through her, but the gratification was short-lived. Inflicting suffering was as ugly as enduring it.

For a while Antony sat so still that, had she closed her eyes, she could not have detected his presence. Then, in a voice which aged in just those few minutes, he said, "I see. Well, this dinner is getting cold."

He handed her a chicken leg wrapped in a napkin. "Now, tell me what had you so worried when you called last night."

"Another of our residents almost died. He is a frail old man who claims someone pushed him into the water. I got to thinking about the police coming around asking more questions. I just couldn't face another interrogation. I couldn't."

Antony shifted closer and put his arms around her. Soon her body shook with silent sobs.

Minnie And The Manatees

"Min, you could get a lawyer," he whispered. "Do you want me to find a good one?"

"God, no," she blurted. "I don't want to talk to another person on earth about this."

"Did the man see who pushed him?"

Minnie shook her head.

"Maybe he just fell, and was embarrassed to admit it, and no police will show up at all."

Minnie pulled back and looked into Antony's face. "Would a person make up something like that?"

He wiped a tear from her cheek. "We men can be pretty stupid when our ego is at stake."

"From the horse's mouth," she said.

He planted a quick kiss on her forehead before she could duck away.

At 12:05 the next day Catherine settled into the chair opposite Minnie for her lunch hour appointment. She presented her hands, then leaned close and asked, "Minnie, have the police been around at all? About Mr. Broomfield, I mean."

"No, thank goodness. Perhaps they don't believe anyone pushed him."

"I hadn't thought of that."

"Antony, my ex, suggested it. It makes me feel a bit better."

"I guess anything's possible."

"Have you heard from your fellow?"

"Yes. Turns out he had an excellent excuse for not calling me." Catherine's voice carried an edge which made Minnie look into her friend's face, but Catherine simply shrugged and offered nothing more.

A blonde head suddenly appeared at Minnie's elbow and a youngster's curious eyes looked up at her. "Where did you get all those colors?" she asked.

"Amanda," her mother called. "Don't bother the ladies." Mother sat across the aisle, her hair layered with foil envelopes containing bleach.

"It's no problem," Minnie answered quickly. "She's fine."

While working on Catherine's nails, Minnie turned to the girl. "The beauty supply house has hundreds of colors. Which one do you like?"

Pale blue eyes ran back and forth over the rows. Finally she pointed to an iridescent pink. "Could you do mine?"

Minnie looked over to the girl's mother, raising her eyebrows. The mother shrugged.

"When my client, Catherine, goes back to wash her hands I will paint your nails."

Grinning, Amanda returned to the waiting area, but before she got too far Minnie managed to just touch her golden hair.

Catherine leaned in to whisper. "Minnie, you're eyes are glistening."

"I'm so sentimental about kids. I love them and don't get that many chances to talk to them. Antony and I were not lucky that way, and I sure didn't expect to be living among so many old people so soon."

Minnie And The Manatees

"Did you ever think about adopting?"

"I would have, but Antony didn't want to. I didn't blame him; it's a tough decision. Didn't you tell me your friend had a son?"

Catherine nodded.

"How old is he?"

"Fourteen. I've only seen pictures of course, since I'm not supposed to exist in Mike's life. His name is Adrian and he has Down Syndrome."

"Oh, that's rough," Minnie said, turning back to her job. "I had a cousin like that. I spent a lot of time with her through her teenage years. I was older, and used to think of it as babysitting but it wasn't that. Serena loved company and just needed a little direction. She was as sweet as a person could be. Kind, gentle and enthusiastic about so many things. Unfortunately her heart was weak, and she didn't live to see her twentieth birthday."

"I can't imagine what would happen to Mike if Adrian died."

"I'm sorry. I didn't mean to scare you. These children are living longer all the time I think the expected life span is into the forties now."

"Mike adores the boy. It's the biggest reason I love him, I think. Nothing else makes much sense."

A silence followed and Minnie rummaged for something to talk about. "Hey, I've got a date," she said.

"Ronald McKay I bet."

"What makes you think so?"

"I was showing property one day when you two were walking by. I waved and neither of you even noticed me. You wouldn't have noticed an elephant in a pink tu-tu."

"It is Ronald. Dinner and then a swing band concert. I may even get a new dress."

"Get something swishy, Minnie. And dangly earrings. Sweep him off his feet."

"You think?" Minnie asked.

"He seems like such a nice man. Why not?"

12

The salesperson was only trying to be helpful, but Minnie was ready to rap her on the head with a hanger. "I told you I don't wear red," she said, shoving the two-piece crimson back through the crack in the dressing room door.

"Oh, that's right. Let me bring you something in green."

Minnie watched the woman's retreating back—her spine so stiff, her bearing so determined, that lives might have been at stake. Minnie closed the door and reviewed the assortment of garments that already decorated her space: a dressy pant suit with a jacket which wasn't long enough, a blue ankle-length dress that made her look twenty years older, a rust knee-length, a gray sheath. For a moment she let her eyes trail to the mirror, but only for a moment. In that quick glance she saw two well-defined rolls of fat between the bottom of her bra and the top of her panties, then puffy legs above the knee-highs. The sight made her turn her eyes upward to study the ceiling. It consisted of acoustical tile, with small holes marching in bisecting lines. She could discern no cracks or unevenness; she had heard stories about people being able to spy on you in dressing rooms. The stories were probably untrue, especially regarding a respected department store like this, but the possibility unnerved her.

Minnie fingered the gray dress, then, tired of it all, eyed the small triangular bench that straddled one corner of the cubicle. Deciding against trying to sit in such a tiny space, she turned, and once again her eyes caught her reflection. Suddenly the futility of the shopping trip overcame her and she threw her arms in the air in defeat. She put on her blouse and pulled on her black slacks. She would have to dredge something unappealing from the closet.

"Try this one, dear," the saleswoman said, handing a dress over the transom.

Minnie almost refused, but the airy sea-green fabric made her hesitate. She took the dress.

"Let me see how it looks when you're ready."

There were actually two parts: a straight green slip for propriety and a gossamer creation that drifted over it. As the dress dropped over her head and floated around her, she knew she was in trouble. This would cost at least twice what she wanted to spend. When it settled over her body, touching in just the right places and none of the wrong ones, she became beautiful. She moved her shoulders just to feel the caress of the material. The color lit her eyes until she looked at the price tag. Two hundred and forty dollars was three times her budget. She ran a finger along the scooped neckline, outlined in rows of mother-of-pearl sequins that copied her fair complexion. As she walked toward herself, the skirt teased her thighs and flirted with her ankles. Ronald had seen her only in modest clothing. She knew that wearing this would set him off, have him expecting certain things. Well, perhaps it was time.

The swing band concert had Minnie bouncing in her seat, and Ronald seemed to enjoy it, too. He asked if she knew of any places to dance aside from the late-night clubs where the young people went. She didn't but would certainly find out.

As they approached Estero Shores, Minnie braced herself for entering the condo which Jimmy Simm had owned. How ironic that she was about to spend a romantic evening in the home of a man whose demise she might have caused. She wondered if she could even carry it off.

But nothing inside the condo supported her impression of Simm. Ronald McKay had incredibly good taste. Minnie knew all of the units had originally been designed like her own, with a small patch of white tile at the entrance, leading to an expanse of colorless carpet and eggshell walls throughout. However, stepping onto Ronald's tile, a rich cocoa with golden veins, made Minnie

Marlene Baird

wish she had splurged on new shoes as well. The smudges on her heels were surely exaggerated by the floor's perfection. It flowed into the kitchen where the counters bore Italian granite which melded with the stainless steel finish on the stove and fridge. The lighting was recessed, suffusing all the harsh corners. As Ronald prepared to make coffee, in a contraption which apparently dripped the liquid directly into a fancy carafe, he flicked a switch which spotlighted only the area he needed.

"Have you done this decorating?" Minnie asked

"Oh, this place was a mess. Such a beautiful home, and the fellow who owned it couldn't have cared less. Everything was still white, except where it was dirty."

Minnie leaned against a counter. The forest green cupboards wavered just a bit.

"Would you like something sweet? A cookie, or ice cream?" he asked.

"Just coffee," she managed.

She moved into the living room.

"Excuse me a minute, Minnie," Ronald said. "I just want to freshen up."

Minnie concentrated on the room around her. Only one lamp was lit, a spreading saucer-shaped fixture which cast its light upward to the ceiling. Matching sofas, their cushions lush in jungle colors, braced each side of the room. Minnie sat on the edge of one of them, her fingers tracing the thick cotton threads. A massive oval coffee table with curved legs and an inlaid top gleamed in the soft light. Ronald had put some effort into this evening and she wouldn't let Jimmy Simm spoil it.

She rose, walked to the window and parted the drapes. Moonlight silvered the broad expanse of water as far as she could see in either direction. She could have been on the deck of a ship, the water seeming to lap at her feet. She was pulling the cord to open the drapes completely, when Ronald returned.

"What a lovely night," he said, coming to stand beside her. "Let's go outside."

Minnie's patio stopped at the edge of her living room, but Ronald's wrapped around the corner, enveloping the master bedroom. Small tables, settees and potted plants were grouped cozily.

"You have a wonderful sense of style," she said.

"Thank you. For a while I dealt in fine art. Maybe that helped."

"When?" Minnie asked. "I thought you'd always been an architect."

"Many an architect, I expect, is a frustrated artist. I certainly was. While in college I worked for a first-class gallery and that spoiled me. I still can't afford what I'd really like." He looked into her eyes. "In art, that is. In women, I hope she's within reach."

Minnie felt throbbing in the hollow of her neck. She covered the area with her fingers and felt her skin jump. Ronald took her hand away, and kissed the spot.

"Perhaps the coffee can wait," he murmured.

It was odd, pressing her lips against those of someone other than Antony. Ronald's kiss was chaste and tender. Minnie wished it were more demanding, making this more his decision than hers, but he was too polite for that. She was not drowning in desire, only in loneliness, and, with utter clarity of purpose, she pulled him close. Surely her body would quickly catch up with her mind.

Despite the perfectly scripted evening, the love-making tended to be ad-libbed. In the bathroom Minnie tried to slip out of her new dress, but caught her left elbow in the sleeve. She must have groaned a bit as she struggled because Ronald came to her aid and, since contortions were required to protect the delicate fabric in the cramped space, their bodies bumped a few times before either was ready. Against her protestations, he insisted in helping her out of the slip as well. Minnie had not planned on his being anywhere near when she stood with her arms in the air and the rest of her exposed.

And they couldn't seem to get the bed comfortable; the pillows took quite a beating before they were just right. At one point Ronald moaned and admitted to having bursitis in one shoulder, which required some rebalancing. As

Ronald's hands softly caressed her sucked-in stomach, then moved upward to cup her breasts, Minnie suffered agonizing flashes, wondering how it had been for Antony, the first time with another woman. Lust would have carried him, she was sure. Whereas this, her first time outside marriage, was based on a quiet romance with a man a smidgen too gentle. Nonetheless, unless Ronald was an academy award caliber actor, they both, finally, achieved clinical climax.

Minnie woke to complete darkness, embarrassed about having fallen asleep. Not moving, she listened for Ronald's breath. Hearing nothing, she let her hand drift across the mattress. She was alone.

Surely she hadn't snored. Antony used to tease her about it, saying she sounded like a bear in heat. Occasionally, he'd pretend to be a snuffling grizzly answering her mating call, and she'd wake to him nuzzling her. She would giggle, they'd wrestle, the bedding becoming twisted and clumped. Those nights were followed by lazy mornings sitting on the patio, barefoot, with coffee and the early paper.

Sadness plunked itself on her heart, and she felt all her facial muscles go slack.

She heard a click and light flowed in from the living room. Ronald, fully clothed, almost filled the doorway. "Are you up?" he asked. In those few words he managed to sound perturbed, peckish and petty. Or perhaps, she thought, I'm punishing him for not being Antony.

"Just," she said.

"I thought you would want me to wake you."

"Of course."

The cool dampness of the outside air at two-thirty in the morning brought Minnie fully awake. Its texture freshened her cheeks and bare arms. Had she been alone, she might have lingered, but as they walked toward Ronald's car, he seemed to be rushing. In fact, ever since he had come into the bedroom to wake her, his demeanor had been uncomfortably crisp.

"You're moving like you were on fire and heading for water," she said, as he gained several feet on her.

He turned and stopped. "Sorry, Minnie. Rude of me."

He opened the car door for her, slid into his seat, and was quiet during the four-minute drive to her building. Was he regretting their love-making? Minnie bit at her lip. Even though she had misgivings about her own motives, she wanted him to have been pleased. Silly vanity. As soon as he turned off the engine, and before he could jump out to open her door, Minnie touched his arm and asked, "What's wrong?"

"It's nothing." His mouth closed abruptly. Even in the half-light of the street lamp she saw his right temple pulse.

Minnie And The Manatees

"That's not true. Please, be honest with me."

He was definitely searching for words. "Something that happens all the time, I expect."

"What are you talking about?"

He took her hand. "You called me Antony."

Minnie stared into his face. He was completely unlike Antony in every way; that was one of the reasons she wanted to care for him. Surely, even in the throes of passion, she could not have mistaken the two of them. But the disappointment in Ronald's eyes assured her that she had.

She touched his cheek. "I'm so sorry if I did that. You must know it was from years of habit." She smiled. "Besides, I can hardly be held accountable, since you're the first man I've been intimate with since my divorce." Actually, since she had married young, Ronald was only the second in a lifetime, but Minnie sensed that admitting something like that these days diminished one's sexual attraction. "Forgive me?" she asked.

"Forgiven and forgotten." He lifted her hand and pressed her fingers to his lips. Minnie wished he hadn't done that; it seemed theatrical.

13

Since she had cat-napped in Ronald's bed, there was no hope of sleep. Minnie showered and slipped on her oldest and softest robe. The chenille was rubbed off at the pockets and wrists, but it always felt like the touch of an old friend. She made a cup of instant coffee and carried it out to the patio.

All was silent and dark, the moon a mere slice in the sky. Minnie closed her eyes. Just as she filled her lungs with the cool air, a frightened scream ripped the stillness. Minnie's eyes flew open, turning to the direction from which it came—Esther Manolo's building, directly across the waterway. A light suddenly blazed in a condo on the third floor, then was immediately extinguished. She ran inside and dialed 911.

Within seconds she heard the distant wail of a siren and fully comprehended what she had done. She would be the focus of inquiries; the law would soon be at her door again. She stood still for a moment, willing away the fear that gripped

Minnie And The Manatees

her. What an awful way to live. Look at what it was doing to her: making her shake while standing in her own home, keeping her awake nights, often bringing her to tears. Well, no more. She would face it. She would confess and have it done with. Minnie pulled her shoulders severely back and pushed her chin up.

She went back outside as the chorus of sirens grew. Out of the corner of her eye she caught a movement across the waterway, two buildings down from Esther's. Someone, in dark clothes, was running. Her fists clutched as she realized she might have looked just like that when on her own mission. As the person dashed between shadows, she caught only glimpses of what looked like a briefcase swinging in one hand. Just before he ducked out of her view, Minnie had the sense of his being stocky and somewhat awkward. She dialed 911 again.

When the ambulance pulled up across the way, Minnie found she didn't want to watch, so she changed into her slacks, a T-shirt and a cardigan with dancing cats embroidered on the front. The sweater was a gift, one she never wore, but the frivolity of the cats appealed to her now. Perhaps she needed a sense of abandon to help carry out her difficult decision. She simply couldn't spend her life being afraid of the police. After answering their questions about this morning, she would admit her act. That she now had the courage to face it, pleased her. The decision had something to do with sleeping with

Marlene Baird

Ronald McKay—something to do with taking risks. She had almost sleep-walked through the five static years which followed the divorce. It was time to look forward, but she would not be able to do that without clearing up the past.

A long forty-eight minutes later her doorbell rang. Detective Wilkins hadn't combed his hair. It stuck out over one ear, making him seem even younger than he had at his first visit. Was that a flannel shirt under his jacket or pajama tops?

"Hello, again," the detective said, stepping inside.

Minnie tried to smile but he didn't see; he was making his way straight through to the deck.

"Mrs. Zuccarelli, would you please show me where you were standing just before you called 911 the first time? I remember you telling me you are often up at dawn but this morning was especially early." He seemed to expect her to elaborate.

"Couldn't sleep," she muttered.

"Where did you see the interior light flash on, then off?"

Minnie pointed. "The third floor, fourth unit from the left."

He nodded. "That would be right."

They returned to the living room and he sat on the sofa, reading from his notebook.

"Your first call came in at 3:07. Tell me exactly what you saw and heard."

"Is anyone hurt?"

Minnie And The Manatees

"Unfortunately, a Mrs. Logan is dead. Did you know her?"

The tenor of recent happenings, and hearing the woman's scream, had prepared Minnie to expect the worst. Still, she sat heavily in a chair. "Her husband was killed in a storm two years ago. It was one of those freak things you see on all the TV newscasts, where a utility pole crashed down on his car. I didn't know them, but his death was the topic of conversation for a long time. What happened to poor Mrs. Logan this morning?"

"I can't discuss that right now. Sorry." His authoritative voice reminded her she was dealing with the police, and the police dealt in consequences. Her resolve to confess melted somewhat.

"Well, I heard the scream first, then saw the light go on and off."

When she began to talk of the man she'd seen running, they returned to the patio and the detective drew a diagram of the buildings, indicating where she had seen the figure. He asked her several times to try to describe him more fully.

"You definitely feel it was a man?"

"From the build, I think it was."

"Not a woman all bundled up?" This made her shudder.

"He moved awkwardly. Not at all graceful."

The detective closed his notebook. "Mrs. Zuccarelli, your quick response will be a great deal of help to us. Thank you."

As he moved back through the living room she gathered her courage. Keeping her voice strong, she said, "Do you have a moment?"

He turned to her, a question wrinkling his brow.

"Detective Wilkins, how do you feel about manatees?"

He blinked, twice. "Pardon me?"

"Do you think saving the manatees is important?"

"I guess everyone does," he said, taking a step backwards, in the direction of escape.

"Not everyone. I had a neighbor who didn't care at all."

Detective Wilkins spoke gently. "Look, Mrs. Zuccarelli, unless this has something to do with what happened this morning—"

"Will you please sit down again?" she asked, motioning him toward the sofa. The detective hesitated, then sat.

Minnie, feeling a need for human connection as she pleaded her case, sat near him.

"Before I first met you, there was another policeman here asking questions. It was about a boating incident. Do you know the name Jimmy Simm?"

Detective Wilkins sat at attention. "I've heard the name," he said. She sensed caution in his voice; he knew more than he was saying.

Minnie swallowed so hard she could hear it. "Well, I wasn't totally honest with that other young officer."

His eyes were trained on her with more professional intensity than when she had been describing her morning. There was no hope of backing down.

"You see, Jimmy Simm used to live a couple of buildings down, and he would race along the waterway in his boat. One morning I was watching a manatee and her baby. They were just below my deck, swimming near the surface. Suddenly he was there, right over them, those huge motors churning the water. I was sure he had injured them."

The detective seemed, now, to have infinite patience.

"I was in a fit of rage all that day, and that evening I decided to act. When it was fully dark, I lowered myself into his boat. I cut some wires and put water in his gas tank, hoping to keep him from going out again soon."

Minnie expected a response. There was none.

She lumbered on. "Then it was reported that his boat was found, out of commission, and he had apparently drowned in that storm."

The detective simply looked at her. He wasn't making the connection. Was he dim after all? She waited.

Finally he spoke. Surely that wasn't a note of comic disbelief in his voice. "Are you saying that you caused his boat to fail and consequently are responsible for his death?"

Minnie nodded.

"Mrs. Zuccarelli, have you been suffering with this from the day he was reported missing?"

"Terribly." She touched his sleeve. "I'm so sorry; I had no intention of harming him, I just wanted to stop him from careening—"

He put his hand over her own. "I can't give you the details of that case since it is still open, but Mr. Simm was guilty of larger crimes than running over manatees, and had far more powerful enemies than you."

For a second Minnie stared at him. Her ears buzzed and she couldn't be sure she had heard him correctly.

"What do you mean?"

"Your actions had nothing to do with Mr. Simm's demise."

Minnie was stunned for a moment. Then she yelped like a pup and threw her body over Detective Wilkins to give him a hug. As he fell backwards, she wrapped her arms around him and kissed his cheek repeatedly. "Thank you," she said over and over before she became aware of his struggling. She had pinned his arms to his sides, immobilizing him. When she realized what she was doing, she tried to back off of him, but her hands sunk deep between the soft cushions. As he groaned, "Mrs. Zuccarelli, please," she felt the weight of her breasts, her stomach, her thighs against the young man's taut frame. Desperate,

Minnie And The Manatees

Minnie threw an arm over the back of the sofa, giving Detective Wilkins enough wiggle room to slide out from under her. He fell onto the floor.

Scrambling to his feet, he smoothed his clothes. "Always happy to bring good news, but I seldom receive such a response."

Minnie, finally seated upright, buried her face in her hands. Red-hot blood coursed through her, and she thought her skin must be the color of her hair. Looking downward, between her fingers, she could see the toes of the man's tennis shoes.

He said, "That must have been a terrible burden. I wish you'd spoken up sooner."

Slowly, she removed her hands and looked up at him. "I've died a thousand deaths."

His eyes softened. "Well, you've suffered a lot longer than Mr. Simm did."

Minnie could think of nothing to say except more thank-yous, so she remained quiet.

"I don't like to leave you alone," he said.

"Is there some danger?"

"That's not what I meant, though you always want to be careful. But you've had a shock; is there someone you can call?"

She nodded.

He moved toward the door. "Lock up behind me and get some rest."

"Just a minute, detective," Minnie said, rising. She pulled a Kleenex from the box on the side table and rubbed at his cheek. "Lipstick," she said. "I want you to know that I don't make a habit of attacking young men in my living room."

"I'll bet you say that to all the officers," he teased.

Minnie dialed Antony, who made no attempt to disguise his anger at being wakened. "Yeah?"

"It's Minnie."

His voice softened. "Min? It's early, even for you."

"I've got the most amazing news."

"You sound giddy. The manatees are back?"

"I didn't kill Jimmy Simm."

"I'll be damned. How do you know?"

"I've been talking to that detective again. Oh, it's a long story. Let's celebrate."

"I've still got that bottle of champagne."

"I've got orange juice. Mimosas in an hour?"

"I'll be there."

Minnie kicked off her slippers and propped her bare feet on the rail of the patio. Only one police car remained in sight and she shifted her eyes away from it. "Did you ever see such a beautiful morning sky?"

"It's those rose-colored glasses you're wearing," Antony replied.

"I'm never taking them off. I'd forgotten how good life could be."

Minnie did enjoy studying the sunrise, but was also avoiding looking at Antony. When he arrived at her door she had kissed him, purely out of exuberance. But he reacted strongly, grasping her as if she'd come back to him. When she retreated, his eyes dulled for a second. Then he recovered and offered up the champagne with a smile.

"I'm glad to see you relaxed again," he said, mixing her another drink. "But this third incident against people living alone worries me. You're always careful, aren't you? Bolting the door and not going out at night by yourself?"

"Of course. But if Mrs. Logan's death was as dramatic as it seems, I'll feel less comfortable."

"What about getting a dog?"

"If you have a dog all your neighbors hate you. You remember when the Lehmanns lived next door."

"Wasn't that awful?" Antony laughed. "Those overgrown mice would start up whenever we were making love. We might just as well have sent up fireworks."

Minnie grinned, her eyes still on the horizon. No matter how they tried, she and Antony had never been able to be quiet. They would stuff their faces into pillows, hold their breaths, try to picture the mutts with their ears to the wall, but, inevitably, one of them would wake the sleeping sentries and sharp yips would cut the air.

"I could barely meet Susan's eyes the next day," she said. "Maybe that's why they moved."

She heard Antony sigh and murmur, "Wonderful times." Then his chair squeaked as he sat straighter, leaning toward her. "It's such a lovely morning, let's go out in the boat. You can't imagine how peaceful the water is at this hour."

"I'm sorry, I'm so tired, the drinks on top of a sleepless night."

"Soon?" he asked.

She studied his handsome face. It was tight with by anxiety as he waited for her answer.

"Okay, soon."

14

After Antony left, Minnie fell onto her bed and slept soundly. Hours later she put a hand to her hair, finding it matted flat against her head. Sticky dampness under her arms made her wince, then she realized she still wore her clothes, including the cardigan. She peered at the drapes, edged in brilliant light. It must be afternoon and the air conditioning was not turned on.

Sunday was one of her two full days off and she decided to pamper herself. She brought her pedicure materials into the living room and spread a beach towel on the carpet. Sitting on the footstool with her feet in the soaking solution, she absently wiggled her toes in time to an old tune playing softly on the radio. She leafed through a glossy magazine, this time not put off by the leggy female models and their insipid male partners. Glistening lips that spread over a half-page only made her admire the color, and she thought she might buy it. She dried her feet, gave them a lotion massage and picked up a new nail color she had brought home from the shop. Then she noticed its name--Murderous Maroon. Now they've finally gone too far, she thought, and dug into her stockpile of half-empty bottles.

After eating a salad and a tablespoon-sized hot fudge sundae, she applied a facial mask and watched the news for a while, then read. By eight o'clock she was ready for bed again, emotional exhaustion having caught up to her.

Tuesday morning, aqua-exercise day, drill sergeant Sylvia almost popped a blood vessel trying to create some order in the pool. The ladies paid scant attention to her demands, being more intent on pumping Minnie for information. Minnie looked for Ronald, but he was absent.

"You actually saw him running away?" Marge Higgins shouted over three other bobbing heads. Her lipstick was outlined with such precision that her open mouth formed a perfect zero.

The story was creating so much attention Minnie wished she hadn't said a thing. "I saw a man, Marge," she said with as much frost in her voice as possible. "I don't know whether he had anything to do with Mrs. Logan."

"Well we don't have that many men running around here in the dark, with or without a briefcase," Marge retorted.

"I bet he was the one," someone else said. Another woman moved closer to Minnie to add, "You'll be a witness if they ever catch him."

"No I won't. I couldn't possibly recognize him."

"Ladies!" Sylvia shouted, clapping her hands overhead to create a rhythm. "Jumping jacks, come on, come on."

Minnie pretended to be intimidated by Sylvia and pressed a finger to her lips as an excuse to fend off the curious women. Marge was suddenly beside her again. It was hard to believe that Marge's skinny arms had ever been strong enough to propel her over the pommel horse, much less into international competition. "I saw you looking around for Ronald McKay. He's in Denver at a family wedding," she said. "I'm surprised he didn't tell you."

"Oh, he did," Minnie replied. "I'm surprised he told *you*."

Marge haughtily tossed her hair, which didn't move, and squeezed her lips together, which highlighted the wrinkles around her mouth. As her body sliced through the water in the opposite direction, she hissed back at Minnie, "Don't count your chickens missy."

"One, two, three, four," Minnie called after her.

"That's the spirit," Sylvia shouted. "Come on ladies, in rhythm just like Minnie."

After getting the oil changed on her car, serving five afternoon clients, and doing some grocery shopping, Minnie looked forward to a quiet evening. She watched a Columbo movie and was asleep by ten-thirty. When the phone woke her, she glanced at the digital clock. Two forty-seven. Drowsy, she said, "Hello," then heard a raw, husky voice she did not recognize, but would never forget.

"Mind your own damn business, big mouth, or be sorry."

The man hung up with a bang, shocking Minnie further.

She shrank back into her bed, breathless, her stomach cramping. The thickened words, rendered more menacing by an accent she could not identify, played in her head. It could only be one person—the man she'd seen running away. How stupid of her to tell the story in the pool, where anyone could hear.

He had intended to frighten her, and had done so. But what bothered her almost as much as his threat was the insulting way he said "big mouth." The part of her that was scared wanted to crawl beneath the comforter and stay there forever, but the part that was insulted wanted to beat him over the head with the receiver, which she still held in her hand.

15

Minnie let the novel fall to her lap. Though the book had been highly touted, she found the story dippy. It was difficult to relate to someone who looked like a movie star and, though a city girl, had the intelligence to run a massive Texas ranch which she inherited. Minnie wasn't deep into the story yet, but already there were hints that Kristal Grange would come to be loved by the Spanish ranch hands for her good works.

A half dozen novels were strewn about, four from the library and two from Barnes & Noble. They represented Minnie's effort to fill every waking moment since the phone call so that she would not dwell on the man's ugly tone. There had been no follow-up call, but she still feared the ring of the harmless pieces of equipment that sat on her kitchen counter and beside her bed.

When she reported the call to Detective Wilkins, he had asked her to come to the station and fill out a report since he was buried in paperwork. Until she saw his desk, Minnie had no idea how hectic his daily life must be. File folders, a dozen pink phone messages, reference books, computer printouts and two coffee cups littered its surface.

He expressed sympathy regarding her anxiety about answering the phone. "It's common for someone who is threatened to feel intimidated by the mere ringing of a phone for some time," he explained.

When she suggested she change her number the detective asked if she would, instead, agree to have her line monitored.

"You mean bugged?" She remembered how her voice had cracked. Embarrassed, she'd looked around the squad room to see who might have heard. Her foray into Jimmy Simm's boat and the resultant anguish had convinced her she was not made for cloak and dagger stuff.

The detective took down the names of everyone who had been in the pool. "Who else did you tell?"

"My ex-husband, Antony. But he'd never threaten me. And I know his voice very well."

Detective Wilkins sat forward, leaning over his desk. "Mrs. Zuccarelli, I know this is frightening, and we want to help. I doubt you are in any real danger because he must know we don't have an identification. Still, on the off-chance he calls again and we can trace it, that would be invaluable to our investigation. If it will make you more comfortable, we can have a cruiser tour the complex every couple of hours for

Minnie And The Manatees

a while; our presence will be obvious to anyone who is interested."

When she still hesitated, Detective Wilkins added, "To save you answering the phone and being frightened, we'll give you a cell phone to use in the meantime. Just let your friends and family have that number."

Minnie tried the novel again, the small phone sitting beside her on the sofa cushion. Even though it didn't actually ring, but sounded like strangled bees when a call came in, it still made her jump.

Another thought disturbed her, drawing her further away from her book. She still hadn't heard from Ronald. Even if he was in Denver as Marge had said, he might have called. But what could she expect, sleeping with a man after a couple of dates, and at her age, when success could hardly be predicted. Perhaps he was sorry it ever happened. She would have liked to get her back up and say that she regretted it too, but she didn't. Even if Ronald did not become an important part of her life, she now knew that sex might. The experience made her feel more vibrant than she had in years. If she were younger, might she become a loose woman? Lovers here, admirers there? She decided these romantic novels served a purpose; they set one's imagination soaring.

Minnie made a tuna salad for lunch, not allowing herself to include a buttered roll, though she thought of biting into one with each mouthful.

Marlene Baird

She sat at the kitchen counter, forcing her attention on her book as she ate. Kristal Grange was breaking a horse, her long legs a decided advantage when trying to stay upright. When the horse threw Kristal, Minnie's interest picked up. Just as the ambulance arrived to sweep Kristal away, Minnie's kitchen phone rang, making her rise straight up off the stool.

She stared at it until the fourth ring, then, thinking of being invaluable to Detective Wilkins, picked up the receiver with her thumb and two fingers as if it were an activated hand grenade.

"Hello?" she squeaked.

"Hi gorgeous," Ronald said. "I've missed you. Been thinking a lot about our last date."

Minnie almost collapsed in relief, then blushed down to her toes. Dear God, don't let him say anything more. She pictured three hard-edged policemen listening inside a van that read "City Laundry & Uniform" on its sides. One would probably be a coarse undercover guy, unshaven, wearing a knitted cap like her own.

"I can hardly believe you missed me when you didn't tell me where you were going and haven't called for days." It was actually more than a week, but she was not letting on that she'd been counting.

"That was thoughtless, but it really was a last-minute thing. My niece got married, giving my brother only two days' notice."

Minnie And The Manatees

Minnie debated about mentioning that he had found time enough to tell Marge Higgins, but decided against it. Why give the cops a chuckle?

"Then," he continued, "since the family was together, which seldom happens, we all went to his cabin in the mountains. Time just slipped away. I really am sorry. Can I make it up to you with a lobster dinner?"

Perhaps it was because of the bits of tuna stuck in her teeth, but neither lobster nor Ronald appealed to Minnie at that moment.

"I have to run. I'll call you," she said, hanging up.

Minnie rinsed her dishes and curled on the sofa with her book, but couldn't get back into it. Judging from the attention Kristal was receiving from a young doctor, she was beautiful and brave even when suffering great pain.

Guilt at being so abrupt with Ronald nagged at Minnie. It was not like her. She put it up to being on edge over her phone being bugged, and wandered to the kitchen. Nibbling on pretzels, she looked out the window. What little she could see of the blue sky was fading, the lowering sun tinting only a few wispy clouds. Tomorrow morning should be clear and calm for her long-promised outing on Antony's boat. He had assured her there would be little rough water, and he would return to land whenever she wished. She had succumbed to his pleas because for some reason this was very important to him, but her knees turned to jelly at the thought.

16

Minnie removed her floppy-brimmed hat and stretched out on a new chaise lounge. There was barely room for it on the boat among Antony's fishing poles, rolled nets and dented metal lockers. She squirmed against a ridge of canvas which pressed into her back. The chair was so recently out of its box that the material buckled where it had been folded. Its stark turquoise and white stripes contrasted with the bleached, peeling woodwork on the inside of the boat.

Antony perched on a built-in bench, the little finger of his right hand controlling the wheel. He had asked her not to call it a steering wheel. They drifted along at about five miles an hour, the soft chug-chug of the motor and its reverberations lulling Minnie. Except for the smells of dried fish and musty salt water trapped somewhere she might have slept.

"This overcast feels good," she said. "I don't have to worry about my freckles."

Marlene Baird

"Unfortunately this will burn off. How about a coffee?"

Holding the wheel in place with his knee, Antony poured two coffees from a fat thermos. Minnie noted that he had added cream for her sake, even though he didn't care for it.

They moved quietly in a wide channel edged by residences. Boats of various sizes bumped the private docks which were manned only by pelicans. The birds hunched languidly on tops of pilings, their folded wings drooping. Expansive lawns led Minnie's eyes toward the homes. No signs of life blinked from windows this early; the morning belonged to Antony and her and the birds. The development had probably been built in the fifties so the houses were not elegant by today's standards but the trees, foliage and flowers had established park-like grounds.

"Is this one of your usual routes?" she asked.

"No. This is a short cut to our destination. I didn't think you would want to be out too long."

Minnie leaned up on one elbow to take a few sips of her coffee. Then she put the cup on the bottom of the boat. She didn't know what to call it but was pretty sure it wasn't a floor. She leaned back again and closed her eyes. Stepping into the boat earlier, gripping Antony's arm, she had fought a rush of fear. What was it about water that frightened her so? She often imagined how wonderful its buoyancy must feel if one could just relax into it. She envied people who could dive and snorkel; those fabulous experiences were impossible for her. But Antony had been patient with her and was so careful to keep the boat level that she was beginning to feel more secure.

A breeze ruffled the hem of her sundress as they left the canal and rounded a jetty of huge rocks. "We're into the gulf now for just a few minutes," Antony explained. "It might be a little choppy."

Minnie swallowed hard and sat up. She adjusted the back of the chaise and gripped the edge of the boat. As Antony accelerated, the bottom of the boat thudded as the hull cut across waves.

He watched her face. "Okay?" he asked.

Holding blowing hair out of her eyes, she nodded.

"Just a bit of this and we'll be in calm waters again. I have to speed up here or we'll be tossed around much more."

They hugged the shore for five minutes and then Antony turned into a sheltered bay. Again, they chugged quietly along, now on the fringe of an industrial area. They looked at the backs of paint shops, body shops, a storage business with dozens of orange-doored cubicles, a metal reclamation operation where crushed automobiles were stacked three high. Then Minnie saw two towers of a Florida Power and Light generating plant rising thirty feet straight up from the shoreline.

Antony slowed even more. "Can you turn your chair around?" he asked.

Minnie shook her head. He cut the engine and they drifted toward the power plant. She looked to Antony for an explanation, for this was hardly an attractive place to stop. Smiling, he pointed over her right shoulder. Minnie twisted to follow his direction and gasped when she saw more than a half dozen manatees playing a couple of hundred feet away. She got off the chaise and kneeled at the side of the boat. Snouts poked out of the water, then she saw the fat roll of a belly, then a flipper. "Oh, Antony," she whispered, not taking her eyes from the scene. Then she pointed. "Oh, there's a young one."

The manatees jostled one another, snuffed on the surface of the water, submerged and rose. They spoke to one another in short squeaks.

"Why are they all here? And how did you know?"

"The power plant returns clean warm water to the bay. They love it."

Then Minnie frowned as one large manatee turned just below the surface and she saw a long white scar on its side. "That one is hurt." Her hand went to her mouth. "Oh, Antony, look," she said through her fingers. He hunched beside her and they watched the gray body drift slowly away from them. As the manatee rolled, his right flipper rose above the surface. Several feet of heavy fishing line and a length of knotted rope were wound around it. Minnie's breath caught.

Minnie And The Manatees

Then she cried, "Oh, my God," as she saw the crab trap, attached to the rope, being pulled along behind. The wire mesh trap frothed across the surface for a moment before the manatee dove, dragging it under.

Minnie hid her face in her hands.

"He's up again," Antony said. "Over there."

Minnie jerked upright. "Can you radio for help?"

"No, Min. I'm sorry. It's out of commission."

"Well, we have to do something. Go over to one of those businesses."

"The shoreline here is off limits. By law I'm really too close now."

Minnie stared him down. "I have a working relationship with the law. Go over to one of those businesses."

Antony put the boat as close as he could to the rocky shore and jumped out. Water sloshed to his knees as he waded in and tied the boat to the limb of low-growing, rangy tree. As he scrambled up the bank, Minnie shouted, "Hurry."

She had a poor view of the manatees from the landing place, so she gingerly stood up. The boat rocked until she was stable. "Don't go away," she called to them. "Don't go away."

Antony returned within a few minutes and pushed off.

"What did they say?" Minnie asked.

"A rescue boat will be out as soon as possible. They didn't promise a time. There is nothing we can do but hope he sticks around."

Once they had returned to their original spot, Minnie strained her eyes trying to find the damaged animal. Then the crab trap bubbled along the surface again and she pointed. "There! But it's going away from the group. Antony, go around. We can herd him back in."

Antony made a slow, wide swing. They were several hundred feet away from the main body of manatees when Minnie spotted the injured one again. "I see him," she said, balancing on wide-spread feet. "What's in that cooler you brought on board?"

"Ham sandwiches."

"With lettuce?"

"And mayo. Just the way you like them."

"Get as close as you can."

Minnie dug into the cooler, carelessly disassembled the sandwiches and pulled out the lettuce. She rubbed some of the mayo onto a napkin and tossed a piece into the water.

The snout of the manatee surfaced almost immediately and he slurped in the lettuce leaf. "Good boy," Minnie said. He submerged and rolled and poked his face up again. She made him wait; she had little food. He shifted his head as if losing interest so Minnie tore a section off one leaf and gave him that. They played the teasing game—she withholding food, he threatening to leave. By the time the lettuce was gone, she had named him Hercules and had managed to touch him once.

"Oh, I want to jump in and hold him," she said.

Hercules submerged for several minutes and Minnie became frantic. Then she saw him rise on the opposite side of the boat, heading still further away from the others. "Why won't he stay put? Antony, go around again."

But before Antony could approach, Hercules dived and they lost sight of him.

Antony circled cautiously. For almost an hour they searched the water, Minnie silently cursing at the rescue people who were being so slow. Intermittently, tears rolled down her cheeks, wetting the top of her dress.

"I can't stand it any more," she said finally. "Let's go home."

Antony turned the boat back toward the gulf. The sun, now free of the morning overcast, sat heavily on their shoulders. "Put your hat back on, Min," he said. But she sat on the deck, knees pulled up under the skirt of her dress, with her pink and puffy face buried in her hands.

"I wish I'd never seen it," she mumbled between her fingers. "That poor creature."

Antony pulled a second thermos from his canvas bag and poured some cold water. He leaned over and nudged her arm so that she would take it. She glanced up at him with eyes so full of misery that he was transported back in time. The memory of her face, twisted by anguish on another day, made him look away for an instant. Then she took the water and drank it down. He put the plastic cup back into the bag and opened the throttle.

There were times during his affair with Barbara when he had envisioned the scene that would play out should Minnie learn of his deceit. He pictured her flaring with anger, certainly in tears, perhaps cursing and striking him. He had told himself that once she had some time to recover he would beg her forgiveness; beyond that his imagination would not go. Blinded by hope, he had never seen her abandoning him, had never anticipated the divorce and his abject loneliness. But neither had he even guessed at the extent of the damage done to Minnie.

They left the sheltered bay and entered the gulf where endless rows of whitecaps laced the water's surface. Antony glanced at Minnie to see if she was concerned that the boat rocked and jerked, but she didn't respond. She had shifted so that her back was to him as she watched the wake. In the stark sunlight her hair took on a brassy hue, an unnatural shade of red, reminding him of the day of the confrontation.

That morning the air was sharp and fresh, and he had just spent a happy couple of hours hand-washing and polishing the Caddy. He and Barbara had parted ways almost a month earlier. Freed from the passion which had stolen his dignity, he felt like a man reborn to decency.

Minnie And The Manatees

During those last few weeks with Barbara, when her grip on him began to slip, he thought often of Minnie and how he could end it all before she found out. If fate would grant him that, he would ask nothing more than to spend the rest of his life pleasing her.

As soon as he entered the condo that day, whistling softly, he smelled the fumes and knew Minnie was coloring her hair.

"Min?" he called, moving toward the bedroom.

She sat on the edge of the bed dressed in an old robe, a stained towel draped around her shoulders. Her hair was sculpted into a spiral cone, cemented in place by chemicals. The telephone dented the pillow, her hand resting on the receiver which sat in its cradle. She was turned from him, staring at the wall.

Antony approached with a sense of foreboding. "It's a fabulous day," he said. "When you finish your hair, let's go for a drive."

She turned her upper body and looked up at him. He noticed that the knuckles on the hand which gripped the receiver were white.

"Min, what's happened?"

She stared at him, right through his pupils and deep into his guilty soul. He could not speak, and he felt his facial muscles broadcasting his fear. Devastation overtook the sweetness of her face. Her eyelids drooped like those of an old woman; her mouth went slack with shock.

Antony's entire body felt chilled at the memory. Coming out of his reverie, he realized the boat was rocking, he had moved a few degrees off course. He corrected, then removed his sunglasses and rubbed his eyes. It was not the first time he felt tears, and he knew it would not be the last.

17

Catherine James was at her desk when she heard the bell, indicating that someone had entered the sales office. She moved through her doorway and saw a man about her age, dressed casually. She automatically went into assessment mode and decided he was not here to buy a home at Estero Shores. He was dressed well enough—his khakis boasted a sharp pleat and his clean tennis shoes were not the old lace-up style, but closed with a Velcro tongue. Still, her instincts told her he was not a customer.

She offered her hand. "Hello, I'm Catherine James. Can I help you?"

When he smiled she caught the unmistakable hint of sexual attraction as he looked at her. This happened almost every time she met a man for the first time. In the business it could be a curse because it sometimes aggravated the wife, who often made the ultimate purchasing decision. But this man had no female companion.

"I'm Detective Wilkins, Fort Myers police," he said. His free hand produced a leather-bound badge from his jacket pocket.

Catherine released his hand and moved back toward her office. "We can talk in here," she said. "I assume this is about Mrs. Logan."

She motioned the detective to a visitor's chair and sat next to him, then waited. He hesitated, simply looking at her, and she became aware that once again a personal interest was interfering with his purpose.

He blinked a couple of times, then began. "Uh, how well did you know Mrs. Logan?"

"Hardly at all. From the office I saw her come and go in her silver Lincoln, sometimes several times a day. I was very sorry, though, to hear of her death."

"I understand that you will be handling the sale of her condo."

"Yes, once the probate is completed."

"Do you sell all the condos that come on the market in this development?"

"Owners are free to choose any real estate agent they want. But I think I'm in the best position to make a sale, and many of them feel that way."

"How did you come to handle Mrs. Logan's place?"

The detective's voice had developed a clipped cadence and Catherine realized he had overcome his attraction to her; he was all business now.

"Her executor called me. He's an attorney; I have his card." It happened to be lying on her desk and she handed it to him.

He glanced at it. "I know that firm."

He relaxed back into his chair.

"What is it you want to say?" she asked.

The detective sighed and leaned forward. "This is awkward. You must understand that I'm not implying that you are involved in any way in the unfortunate deaths here. It's just that the only link we can find between the recent victims is that you have sold their properties, or, in this case, are about to."

Catherine frowned. "And?"

"So far as we can tell, you're the only person who has gained anything in each case."

Catherine felt the color leave her face, and smiled to camouflage the fact. "Even though you deny it, that sounds like an indictment of some kind."

"Really, Mrs. James—"

"I'm not married." She saw his eyebrows rise an eighth of an inch which caused her to recross her legs. Old habits die hard.

"Ms. James . . . I only mention the coincidences in the hope that you might be able to shed some light . . . I mean, I thought perhaps you had come by the opportunity for the sales through a single source."

"I can tell you about recent sales. When Jimmy Simm died I contacted his family because he had told me where they lived. Then, Esther

Manolo's daughter approached a friend of mine, Minnie Zuccarelli, and Minnie recommended me to her. And this time it was the attorney."

"And what about Gregory Barnes?"

Catherine was stunned. "Gregory? He drowned in the pool months ago. Surely there's no connection."

"In light of the other deaths here, we are taking another look at Mr. Barnes's situation. Did you sell his place?"

His tone told her that he already knew the answer to the question. "Yes," Catherine said, sensing that the earth was, if not opening under her, at least cracking.

He looked directly into her eyes for a full ten seconds. Catherine refused to blink. Was he trying to read her thoughts, hoping to find guilt among them? Whatever his intent, he suddenly seemed satisfied and hoisted himself from the chair. He put out his hand. "I appreciate your time, Ms. James."

"Catherine," she offered, only slightly ashamed of herself for taking advantage of his interest.

His fingers lingered in her hand, then he moved quickly from her office.

Catherine didn't sleep that night. Her conversation with the detective had aroused a discontent she'd been trying to suppress. Just as a wind storm can make a weapon out of a grain of sand, her churning thoughts gave weight to latent suspicions. She needed to talk it through with someone and decided to visit Minnie the next evening after work.

Minnie was scanning the newspaper when the doorbell rang. Peering through the fish-eye she saw it was Catherine.

"Have you got a few minutes, Minnie?" Catherine asked, when invited inside.

Minnie suggested they sit in the living room but Catherine preferred to stand, so they hovered near the kitchen counter, which Minnie found uncomfortable. Catherine, in a blue pantsuit, looked tired and picked nervously at her nails as she spoke. "The entire place is buzzing about Mrs. Logan, and I've heard several different versions of what happened. Two people told me that the police were at your door."

"Only because I called 911. I was up late, out on the patio, and heard Mrs. Logan scream. Poor woman. The detective wouldn't give me any details, but it sounded to me like she was terrified."

"Gossip has it that Mrs. Logan's death was a robbery gone bad. Apparently she had some expensive jewelry."

"Oh, I wouldn't know about that, except . . . ."

"What, Minnie?" Catherine urged.

"I saw a man running between the buildings a bit later."

"I heard about that. Do you think he was involved?"

"Who knows? I thought he had a briefcase in his hand but if it was some other kind of a bag, like a satchel, perhaps it *was* a burglary. For once I'm glad I have nothing worth stealing."

"What did he look like, the man who was running?"

"Stocky, didn't move very fast."

"Can we sit down?" Catherine asked suddenly, and Minnie saw that she had gone pale.

Minnie pointed to the stools at the kitchen counter and Catherine slid onto one of them. She dropped her head and sank all her fingers into that thick hair, pulling it fiercely back from her face. Minnie saw sharp angles and stress lines she'd never noticed before. "What's the matter?"

Returning her hands to her lap, Catherine faced Minnie. "Do you know a detective named Wilkins?"

"I think he's just a doll," Minnie said. "Did he interview you?"

"He has a theory that has to do with motive. Since I've sold all the condos that have come vacant, he has concluded that I'm the only person who has benefited from the deaths. He even questioned me about the sale of Gregory's place."

"You must have misunderstood. Surely, he didn't accuse you."

"Not exactly. But he planted some ugly suspicions in my mind, and now I don't know if I'm crazy or just plain scared."

Minnie could not fathom what Catherine was getting at. "For Heaven's sake, what's bothering you?"

Catherine reached for Minnie's hand. "Can I swear you to secrecy?"

"Of course."

But Catherine still hesitated. She took a shaky breath. "You remember me telling you about my friend Mike?"

Minnie nodded.

"He told me about a troubled past, and he admitted some things about his lifestyle that disturbed me. It left me doubting him." She held up her hand cautioning Minnie not to misunderstand. "Not doubting my feelings for him. But I realize I don't know him." She paused. "And I think he might be capable of violence."

Minnie jerked upright, her hand coming free of Catherine's. "He didn't hit you."

"No, no. He wouldn't," Catherine assured her. "But I wonder if he might not hurt someone else in order to help me." The younger woman's eyes pleaded for Minnie to assure her she was talking nonsense.

Minnie almost laughed it was so absurd. "You mean Mike is doing away with people to provide you with income? Now that's just plain nuts. Why wouldn't he just give you money?"

"Because I won't take it." Catherine slid off the stool and paced. "Minnie, because of Mike's being married, you're the only person I've talked to about him. You don't know how impulsive he can be, and he's overly protective. What do you think, am I completely crazy?"

"Unless you can explain to me why you think he's violent, I think you are."

Catherine stopped pacing and spoke deliberately. "Remember when I was so upset because he wasn't calling me?"

Minnie nodded.

"Mike beat a man with his fists so hard that they put him in jail."

Minnie kept her face even, although her insides were cringing. How had Catherine managed to get involved with such a man?

Catherine continued. "He admitted to being in trouble with the police as a youngster, but I just know he hasn't told me everything. Why would he?"

Why, indeed, Minnie thought. But how could Minnie judge Mike? She had never even laid eyes on the man . . . or had she? Could someone be that foolish? Desperate enough to murder innocent people? No, she couldn't accept it. And certainly her friend needed comfort now.

"Isn't this the same man who loves his son so much? Surely he would never do anything so stupid when the boy relies on him."

Catherine seemed to weigh Minnie's words, then some of the anxiety left her face. "That

Minnie And The Manatees

makes sense. He would never jeopardize Adrian's future."

With Catherine settling down, Minnie suggested a cup of coffee.

"Thanks, Minnie, but I've got a lot to think about. You've been a wonderful friend. I can't thank you enough." She walked to the door and opened it, then closed it again. "You won't say anything about my stupid suspicions?"

"Of course not," Minnie said.

Marlene Baird

18

As Minnie leaned over the sink finishing her dinner dishes, an ache spread through her upper back. She shrugged her shoulders up under her ears, held them for a few seconds and dropped them quickly. The tension eased, but within minutes the contraction returned. She knew it was because of Hercules. Since seeing him, her entire body had felt as tight as if it were wrapped in steel. And then had come the conversation with Catherine. Though she had been quick to allay her friend's fears about Mike being involved, Minnie found herself trying to recall, exactly, the voice of the man who had threatened her over the phone. When she first told Detective Wilkins of the call he had asked her if the man had any kind of accent, and she told him that he did. And yet, when pressed to suggest its origin she was at a loss. "Well then," the detective had suggested, "perhaps it was a fake, someone disguising his or her voice so you wouldn't recognize it." That possibility had not

Minnie And The Manatees

escaped Minnie, but she could think of no one in her circle of acquaintances who could possibly be involved or be so cruel as to make a call like that. But Mike was not in her circle, and he could have learned many details about Estero Shores from Catherine.

Minnie realized she had stopped moving and was standing with her hands in cooling water. A soapy scum had formed around her wrists. She drained the sink, ran more hot water and completed her job. What she needed was a long aromatic soak in the tub to remove these thoughts from her mind. She had only used a quarter of the fat jar of lavender salts which had been a Christmas gift from Antony's sister, Marie.

Minnie sank into the warm, scented water and waited for contentment to arrive. She waited for at least ten minutes, eyes closed and breathing deeply. When her body remained so stiff she could barely stay folded into the oblong tub, she reached for the squat jar. "Essentiel Elements, de la rue Verte," it read. Essential elements of the green street? That didn't seem right. "Joie de Lavender," it continued, "Aromatherapy Bath Salts." Then came the promise: "Calming and Purifying."

Turning on the hot faucet with her toes, Minnie felt the stream of heat snake around her body. She sank deeper and tried to clear her mind, but it simply wasn't going to work. Clearly these aromatherapy products had not been tested on a person who had recently heard coarse words spit at her over the phone, then had seen, up close, one of God's gentlest creatures crippled, followed by the burden of entertaining grave doubts about a friend's lover. She felt such a tangle of emotions—fear, anger, sympathy, guilt—that she could not concentrate on dispersing one without the other popping up.

While she put on her nightgown and creamed her face the question nagged at her. Could that voice possibly have been Mike's? As she walked through the condo, double-checking that the coffee pot was turned off, dousing lights and locking the patio door, she decided again that no one could be so desperate to help a loved one that he would harm innocent people. But as she slid into bed and clicked off the bedside lamp, she recalled her own desperate days and realized that even she was capable of temporary madness.

She had been sitting on the edge of this same bed when she answered the phone and learned that Antony had cheated on her. She recalled twisting a corner of the old green satin spread in her hand. Antony had loved that spread, which, within a few hours of the call, had been dumped in a box headed for the Salvation Army. That day, that awful moment, her hair was mounded into a gooey mess on her head and she dabbed at dripping places with a badly stained towel which was draped over her shoulders.

Minnie And The Manatees

"Minnie," the voice on the phone had said, "this is Marge Higgins. We met a couple of times when you first moved in."

"I remember," Minnie said, not in the mood for conversation with this woman. In just two meetings Minnie had found Marge pushy and snide, and she loved nothing as much as attention.

Minnie stopped a drip from trickling down behind her ear. "What is it Marge?"

"Well, this is difficult. I hardly know where to start."

"Just say it. I'm coloring my hair."

"Oh, should I call back later?"

Minnie wanted to get it over with. "No, go ahead."

"Okay. I was talking to a friend of mine this morning who knows a woman named Barbara Coulter. Do you know her?"

"No."

"Well, Barbara told my friend about this man she had been seeing recently, and, without a doubt, the man was Antony."

What was this woman babbling about? "What do you mean? Was she implying a relationship or something?"

"I think so."

"Well, you've got it wrong. That's nonsense."

"But, it isn't, Minnie."

"Why would you say such a thing?"

"I'm sorry, but she described him perfectly, right down to the pink Caddy."

The whole world went still for Minnie. Her attention wandered, her thoughts scattering, escaping the voice. The sound of the clock radio clicking over to four o'clock cut sharply into the humming that ran through her head. Slowly she became aware that Marge was still talking.

"Us gals have to stick together. I sure would want to know about something like this if it happened to me."

Minnie slammed the receiver into its cradle, fighting the urge to snatch it up again and ask for more details. Then her groping mind found a detour, a way around the disaster. Marge was a stupid woman. This was some kind of spiteful prank, a high-schooler's idea of revenge. But what axe did Marge have to grind with Minnie? She was digging desperately for an answer when she heard Antony enter the condo, whistling.

As he approached the bedroom, she turned to the wall to regain her composure. When he entered the room he said something about going for a drive. She hadn't decided whether to mention the phone call when he said, "Min, what's happened?" Every hair on Minnie's arms rose, because his halting voice registered fear, as though he had an inkling of what the bad news might be.

She turned to face him. His mouth pinched, and the crease between his eyebrows deepened. She stared into his eyes and they clouded over, as though to block her view. She clutched the towel; it was true.

Even so, even if it were true, she had to give him one chance. "Who is Barbara?"

Antony said nothing.

Lie to me, she pleaded silently. *Lie to me.*

But Antony went pale. His body swayed, and she thought he might crumple to the floor.

Now, lying under the new spread, Minnie remembered all those nights drowning in tears as she tried to sleep. She hadn't been able to get dressed for five days.

When the hurt was raw, it shut off rational thought, and reason gave way to blinding anger. At those times she had felt capable of doing physical harm to Antony and to the woman. What might she have done had she been a strong man like Mike instead of a defeated wife?

Tears burned behind her eyes. Her choice of words—a defeated wife—had brought them. Most of the time she no longer thought of herself that way, but occasionally the vulnerability would creep in and the sting would return. Minnie remained flat on her back, hands at her sides, blinking the tears away. She would not allow more than a moment of self-pity. To succumb would invite sorrow and frustration and even second-guessing. Should she have forgiven Antony? Many women had done as much and seemed content. He had been truly repentant, and she had never doubted his love for her. But she could not forgive, and she had learned that pride has the power to strengthen. Pride can stiffen the spine.

Minnie got out of bed and made a cup of tea. Not soothing chamomile, but dark, strong Earl Grey, the kind the Brits drink, she thought, when they have to face a day of drizzle seeping down the necks of their slickers. And she decided she would call Ronald in the morning.

19

Minnie glanced at the wall clock, an art-deco creation encased in pink plastic. Seven minutes yet. Due to the owner's excellent taste, the entire shop sparkled in chrome, black and pink and yet managed to evoke a sense of business. She straightened the rows of polish on her table then retrieved a Diet Pepsi from the small fridge back near the shampoo bowls, wishing she had some whiskey with which to spike it. Valerie Germond was Minnie's last client of the morning.

One of the hair dressers whispered to Minnie as she passed by, "Take heart. Maybe she won't show up." Minnie toasted the thought with a raise of her Pepsi can.

Then Valerie Germond burst through the front door, addressing everyone with a flourish. "Sorry I'm late. Hate to keep you waiting." She had not inconvenienced a single one of them, yet, but the thought seemed to appeal to her.

Marlene Baird

Despite the woman's cheerful demeanor, within minutes she would be burying Minnie in a vitriolic account of all the shoddy workmanship and insensitive salesclerks she had encountered during the week. Discontent was her lifeblood. At every visit she wanted Minnie to change the shape of her nails from short to long or blunt to round. She spent five minutes choosing a color, only to complain that within days it had become boring. Minnie's bottom drawer held seven odd shades she had bought trying to please Valerie, each of which had been used only once.

It took Valerie three full minutes to settle into the chair opposite Minnie. She always dressed as if, immediately following her appointment, she would be rushing to the docks to board a luxury liner. Layers of beautiful fabric had to be tucked and draped just so before she was ready.

"How are Christopher and Pooh?" Minnie asked, when Valerie finally presented her hands. Mentioning the matching Silky Terriers would delay Valerie's complaining for a few minutes. The woman leaped at the chance to babble on about their latest tricks as Minnie half listened. Minnie's favorite story was one she had heard from someone else. Apparently Pooh was aptly named and was not particular about where he proved the point. One day Valerie caught her husband Stanley smacking Pooh on the rump. The next day Valerie's lawyers slapped Stanley with divorce papers.

". . . and then Christopher, the little devil, chewed up that pillow just so Pooh couldn't play with it. Can you imagine?" Valerie giggled.

"Not really," Minnie replied, picturing Valerie's ex-husband far away, with a constant smile on his face.

"Let's go square today," Valerie said as Minnie removed the last of the old polish. "Have you read the paper?"

"Not yet." Minnie began to file off the perfect ovals which, for a few weeks at least, had served to lengthen Valerie's stubby fingers.

"They rescued a manatee not too far from here."

Minnie stopped moving, holding Valerie's left hand in mid-air. "When?"

"A few days ago."

"Was he injured, or was he sick?"

"It was a she. One of her flippers was wrapped with ropes or something. It was so badly infected they had to amputate. Must have cost us taxpayers a ton of money."

Minnie saw Hercules, helpless on an operating table, shot with antibiotics and anaesthetic. She dropped her hands, sending the nail file to the floor.

Valerie jerked her hand away as if it might be damaged.

"Will it survive?" Minnie asked.

"Apparently. They've named her Helena."

"I have to go," Minnie said, rising.

Valerie splayed her naked fingers. "But, but—"

Minnie drove far too fast on the way home, tore open her newspaper and found the article. It mentioned the crab trap. She called Antony.

"You won't believe it," she began as soon as he picked up.

"They've rescued Hercules."

"Only he is a she," Antony said.

"Wait, you're not surprised. You knew and you didn't tell me?"

"I've been waiting all day to hear your voice with that ring of happiness."

"What a beast you are. But how wonderful this is."

"I followed up after our outing and learned of the rescue. Then I explained that we had made the call. They said that if the gender had not been wrong they would have named it Hercules just for you."

Two days later Minnie hummed along with the radio as she drove to meet Antony for lunch. She wore a periwinkle blouse which tapered at the waist and sat on her hips. Her long cotton skirt matched white sandals from which brilliant red toenails poked.   After contacting the sanctuary, she had been floating on air. They said Helena's prognosis for recovery was very good and promised to let Minnie know when the

Minnie And The Manatees

manatee was well enough to join the others in the viewing tank.

Antony was just exiting the Caddy when she pulled into a parking spot nearby. For once he was parked alongside everyone else, instead of at the empty end of the lot. He didn't come over to her, but waited. She became self-conscious as he watched her approach.

"Wow," he said, winking.

Minnie blushed.

He took her hand, rubbing her fingers gently. "You look fabulous. And I love this bright red polish." He kissed the back of her hand.

"I'm so happy about Hercules," Minnie said, to diffuse his attentions.

"Helena," Antony reminded her, taking her arm and moving toward the restaurant.

A blast of cold air met them at the door. "Gosh," Minnie said, "I should have brought a sweater."

"Maybe it's warmer in the sunshine," Antony offered.

But even next to the floor-to-ceiling windows, it wasn't, and Minnie hugged herself as she studied the menu. Goosebumps were forming when she decided on lobster bisque. She waved at the busboy. "Can I get some hot coffee, please?"

As she lowered her arm, Antony took her hand again. "Hey, this nail polish isn't red. It's that ugly brown."

"The color changes with the temperature of the air or your body. When I go outside and get into that hot car it will be red again."

"Hard to believe," Antony muttered.

The busboy put Minnie's coffee in front of her. "Watch," she said. She held the nails of one hand against the hot cup for a few seconds. Then she showed Antony the bright red spots on each nail.

"I'll be damned. Who discovered that?"

"Someone who has made a good deal of money since. It's the rage among young girls, and I feel young today."

"Because of Helena."

"And because you were so considerate as to keep in touch with the rescue people. I know you have a different slant on the manatees' importance, so that was sweet of you."

"They're winning me over," Antony said.

Antony ate a salad the size of Mt. Etna and the soup warmed Minnie until she was almost comfortable. They shared a slice of cheesecake. Antony told a couple of funny stories about his fishing buddies, and Minnie relayed the tale of Pooh.

"This Valerie sounds like a waste of your energy."

"I probably won't see her again. After leaving her sitting at my table with half-finished nails, I'm sure I've been relegated to her long list of undesirables." Minnie paused. "You know, there are few people in the world that I don't like."

Her thought was cut off as Antony suddenly twisted his entire upper body away from her. He looked out the window. Minnie followed his line of vision expecting to see a boating accident or other calamity. "What is it?" she asked.

Antony didn't turn, but hissed at her. "Going out. Isn't that Marge Higgins?"

Minnie swiveled around to catch a glimpse of a turquoise skirt with metallic threads sweeping through the doorway. The retreating figure became a dark blob against the outside glare.

"You can turn around now. I don't know if it was her."

Antony slowly resettled into his former position. He shook his shoulders like a dog shucking water. "Do you think she saw us?" he asked.

"Why would it matter?"

"I thought she might come over to say hello to you. I'd have had to restrain myself from belting her."

Minnie almost asked what right he would have to do that, since the crime had not been in her telling, but in his doing, but she let it pass.

"I doubt she'd come over to greet *me*. The only time I see her is in our exercise class, and she has been antagonistic. After she spilled the beans on you all those years ago, she acted as if we were best of friends and treated me like a precious petunia. Then we went back to being just acquaintances, which suited me better. But lately she seems intent on putting me off balance again."

"What about?"

Minnie knew Marge was jealous of Ronald's attentions, but should she mention his name to Antony, putting a face on his fears? When she called Ronald they had made a date for a movie; maybe it was only decent to make Antony aware. "Do you remember asking me if I was dating someone?"

Antony nodded, pursing his lips.

"Well, Marge made a point one day of bragging to me that she had some contact with this same fellow. I have no idea to what extent, but she was rude about it. So far as I know I've never done a single thing to hurt her."

Antony turned his unused coffee spoon over a few times, then polished the bowl on the tablecloth. "We're being brutally honest today," he said.

"I didn't mean to be brutal."

"Marge Higgins is a dolt," he said. "She came on to me, hard, a couple of times many years ago. When I didn't respond she turned ugly." He took a breath and let it out in a long sigh. "I'm sure that's why she told you about Barbara. It was about getting back at me."

Minnie reflected on how different their lives would be if Marge hadn't been so vindictive. "I probably would never have found out except for Marge."

Minnie And The Manatees

"Don't, Min," Antony pleaded. "Don't think about it."

"I don't very often," she said. "But now Marge has turned her anger on me."

"As I see it, once again you've got the attentions of a man she wants. It's no more than that. If anything, you should be flattered. By the way, is he a nice man?"

Minnie nodded but couldn't meet his eyes.

"And you're still seeing him?" Antony's voice almost broke from the strain of trying to sound neutral.

Minnie nodded again, then raised her head. "He and I have no bad history. It's easier."

Antony looked into her eyes until she had to blink. "It must be," he said. He turned to face outside. He set his teeth and his cheeks quivered. Minnie knew she had hurt him and he was fighting his reaction. She almost touched his arm, almost said that Ronald was not someone she loved, but held back. Maybe it was better to create a separation, to finally accept that this relationship, a friendship which renewed pain on both sides, should be abandoned.

After a few moments she asked, "Are you ready?"

Antony picked up the bill, and they left.

When the hot outside air engulfed them, Minnie noticed her nails brighten and wished it were that easy to change her mood. Antony walked her to her car and, as she folded herself into the driver's seat, he kissed her forehead. "Marge was right. You *are* a precious petunia," he said.

She drove away with tears in her eyes. Frustrated, she banged on the steering wheel with her fist. *Damn! Why can't I decide what I really want?*

By the time she neared Estero Shores the tears were falling in fat streaks. So she was never exactly sure where the car had come from. Suddenly it was there, aimed right at her and moving fast. Minnie jerked the wheel of her Camry to the right. Luckily there was no one beside her as she crossed the outside lane and bumped up the curb. She slammed on the brakes at the same time her front left fender smashed into the side of a Plexiglas bus shelter.

20

Minnie arranged placemats, coffee mugs and a plate of cookies on the table; she would not have Detective Wilkins sitting on the sofa where she had attacked him. She topped up the sugar bowl, filled the creamer, then checked her watch. He was only ten minutes late but it seemed like an hour. It had been a gut reaction, calling him, and she was beginning to regret it. Physically and emotionally shaken after the accident, her thoughts had run on the wild side. Now she wished she had not reacted so quickly.

The car had rocked before settling, and Minnie sat a moment, her hands clutching the wheel like claws. Then she jumped out and ran around to the front of the shelter to see if anyone had been inside. It appeared empty. Suddenly a police car pulled up at the curb. The officer's first concern was her condition. She assured him she was fine. After asking her a long series of questions, he pulled her left fender away from the tire and asked her to start the car and back away. Everything seemed to be working.

"You're probably safe to drive home," he said. "That airbag should have popped. Better have it check out."

Minnie thanked him and drove off. It was not until she parked in her spot in the garage that she fell apart. She saw the flash of the car coming directly at her, so directly that she felt it was aimed her way on purpose. Someone trying to scare her? Or someone trying to hurt her. She got out of the car and forced herself to walk the length of the garage a couple of times. The trembling in her limbs lessened. As she rode up in the elevator her mind locked on to one idea. Could the driver have been the man she saw running on the morning of Mrs. Logan's death?

Another ten minutes passed before Detective Wilkins arrived but when he did there was a new crispness about him. The slouchy cotton jacket had given way to a navy blazer. He had a spiffy haircut, short around the ears, which strengthened his jaw line, and loafers replaced his tennis shoes.

"May I come in?" he asked.

Minnie was startled, realizing she had been staring at him. But he really did resemble the male models in the magazines at the shop.

She stepped back so he could enter. "I see why you're late," she said. "Going to a cocktail party later?"

"Oh, the get-up." He rubbed the front of the jacket. "No, just stepping out of character a bit."

She motioned him toward one of the chairs and retrieved the coffee pot.

"None for me," he said.

"You're sure?" she asked, pouring her own.

"I've had plenty today."

As she returned the coffee pot to the warming plate he asked, "How are you doing? You sounded anxious on the phone."

"I'm fine now. In fact, I wish I hadn't called you. It was probably just an accident."

"Let's hope so." He opened a manila folder and removed a piece of paper. "You said the car was fairly new. Can you do any better than that?"

"All the newer cars look the same to me, with their curved fenders."

"But it definitely wasn't an SUV?"

"No, a car. Goldish colored."

"Goldish?"

"Bronze, maybe."

"And you didn't see the face of the driver?"

Minnie shook her head.

"That seems odd," the detective said. "Usually, even in that split second, people have a sense of who was driving. A man or a woman, someone tall or someone short."

"The person did not have a lot of hair, but I didn't see the face at all."

Detective Wilkins twisted his lips as if frustrated but trying to be patient. "Mrs. Zuccarelli, are you absolutely sure about this? I've known many accident victims who remember, above all else, the haunted look on the face of the other driver."

"I was distracted." Minnie bit into a sugar cookie. No way was she going to admit that she'd been crying.

"Distracted by what?"

Minnie's mind raced around possibilities. She had passed a fellow on a bike just before the accident. "A cyclist. I was watching him to make sure he didn't swerve into my lane."

Wilkins looked at her for several seconds. "The police report said you were driving on the inside lane."

Minnie pretended not to hear. "He had on one of those beetle-shaped helmets and bright yellow shorts." Then she closed her mouth to prohibit further lies.

"Mrs. Zuccarelli, I sense that you're evading my questions. Perhaps you recognized this person and don't wish to tell me."

Minnie saw that she was digging herself a hole. "Okay. Here's the truth. I was crying, all right? I was bawling my eyes out. You satisfied now?"

His look of sympathy made her vulnerable again. She pushed away from the table and went to the bedroom.

Minnie And The Manatees

After a minute he called to her. "I'm going to pour myself that coffee now if you don't mind."

Minnie blew her nose, came back and plunked herself in the chair. "I'd had lunch with my ex. Sometimes that makes me cry."

"Then why do you do it?"

"I always think I'm over him."

"Been there, done that," he said.

"A wife?"

"Fiancé. I was so pathetic that she changed the wedding date a half dozen times before I even caught on."

"She could have been more straightforward," Minnie offered.

"That ended over a year ago, and I still find it unnerving. I can't trust that what a women says is what she means. I'm never sure I'm reading things right." He grinned. "Any suggestions for me?"

"Don't rush. Marriage is tough. And don't be so hard on yourself. Even when you think you've found the perfect mate and lived together for thirty years there can be surprises." Minnie dabbed at her eyes then stuck the tissue in her pocket.

"I'm sorry if you're unhappy," the detective offered.

"It comes and goes."

"Are you feeling better now?"

"I'm fine. Are we finished?"

"No. I'm worried about you. You need to think very hard. If this wasn't just a freak accident, there is someone in your life who wants to frighten you, or worse. You *must* have some clue."

She'd had one wild thought. If he was the man she saw running from Mrs. Logan's place, how would he even know who she was? Unless he was Catherine's friend, Mike. In all innocence, Catherine could have told Mike many things about Estero Shores.

Minnie changed her mind about mentioning Mike several times in a moment, then said, "I can think of only one remote possibility, and it is really out of left field."

"Give me anything."

"I've never met this man; this is second-hand and probably means nothing. He's involved with a friend of mine, Catherine James."

"Catherine? The lady in the sales office?" The detective's tone expressed a personal interest.

"She has some doubts about him," Minnie said, watching the man's face. He seemed lost in his own thoughts, which gave Minnie time to measure her own, branding herself a traitor.

When he finally urged her to continue, she said, "There's really nothing more. It's foolishness."

"If it's groundless, it's groundless. Please let me decide. What is his name?"

"I only know his first name. Mike."

"And tell me what brought him to mind."

"Catherine told me he has a shady past. That's all." Minnie put her hand on the detective's arm. "Please don't make any more of this. Catherine is a friend. She swore me to secrecy, and I'm undoubtedly wrong."

"We will be discreet in checking him out."

The detective rose, picked up his coffee mug and carried it to the sink. He called back over his shoulder as if to give his question a casualness. "Is it a serious relationship, this one between Ms. James and this man?"

"Oh, yes," Minnie said, following him, feeling like a pariah for even mentioning Mike's name.

Detective Wilkins turned toward her; somehow in the last few minutes he'd lost some of his GQ quality. "With any luck we'll know within a few days at the most whether this Mike was in that car, and I promise neither he nor Ms. James will be aware of our investigation."

On his way out of the development, Detective Wilkins stopped in front of the sales office. He tried to get a glimpse of Catherine through the window, but the sun hit the glass in such a way that the interior was dim. He had planned to go inside and judge his chances of a date, but there was no reason to do so now. Mrs. Zuccarelli said Catherine's relationship with this Mike was a serious one. Wilkins shucked out of his blazer and pulled onto the main road feeling dejected. That she had a love interest was disappointing, but what could he expect of a beautiful woman like that?

Catherine had dominated his thoughts ever since their interview, and he had made a point to learn her address. It would be easy enough to watch her place for a while and identify this Mike.

He drove slowly back to the station, trying to sort out his motivations, and, by the time he arrived, the man who had swerved into Mrs. Zuccarelli had been identified.

He dialed her cell phone number.

"A balding man in a light brown 1998 Honda crashed into a storefront five miles down the road a few minutes after you hit the bus shelter," he told her. "He had been drinking. His name is Richard Mueller. Ring any bells?"

"Never heard the name." He could sense her relief before she added, "I feel so much better, knowing it wasn't Mike."

"I feel better knowing that whoever he was, he wasn't aiming at you," the detective said. "Take care."

Wilkins chewed at his bottom lip. Except for his personal interest in Catherine James, there was no legitimate reason, now, for him to seek out this Mike person. But Catherine had seemed like an intelligent woman. Why would she be romantically involved with someone with a shady past, as Mrs. Zuccarelli had put it? How shady was he? Could he have something to do with Catherine making all those condo sales? He

Minnie And The Manatees

didn't want to learn that Catherine was part of a conspiracy. He only wanted to charge up on his white horse and save her.

21

"What's his real name again? Billy Bob? Billy Joel?" Minnie asked, dumping her popcorn bag in the trash can. The ending to the movie had been unexpected and thrilling. Everyone in the crowd seemed to be talking as they flowed into the lobby.

Ronald chuckled. "Billy Bob Thornton. This was a different type of role for him."

"You mean he's not usually funny?"

"Heavens no. Just the opposite. Didn't you see *Slingblade*?"

"I guess not. I don't see many movies anymore." Sometimes one of her friends from the shop would suggest an afternoon movie, but Minnie only went along if she was desperate. Antony and she used to catch everything that was worthwhile, and she still associated a dark theater with holding hands and sharing a mood.

She and Ronald stepped out into a balmy, fragrant night.

"Let's walk a bit," Minnie suggested, and they aimlessly strolled westward.

When Ronald took her hand she noted its warmth. He'd been quiet most of the evening, almost checking his words before he spoke. He seemed to be rehearsing something he was not ready to share.

After a full block of silence, Minnie said, "Tell me about your trip home."

He seemed glad to be given a topic. "It really was terrific. The niece who got married is the oldest of four. My brother also has twelve-year old twins, and Nola, a teenager who's attached at the wrist to her cell phone. It got hectic, but I enjoyed it. Do you have any siblings?"

"A younger step-sister in Dallas, but we never got along. We exchange Christmas cards and she sends pictures of her kids. That makes me a little jealous." They were stopped by a red light and, in sync, turned to go back. "Did you ever want to have kids?" she asked.

"I never felt I'd be a good father."

Minnie waited for more, but he lapsed back into his earlier reserve.

Ronald's Buick sparkled under the floodlights of the empty parking lot. Once inside, he made no move to start the car but turned sideways to look at Minnie.

"I've really missed you."

"I wouldn't know it by the flurry of phone calls."

"I didn't know if I should press the issue. I realize that our last date was somewhat disappointing to you."

Minnie sensed he was referring to the love-making and began to inject a denial, but he stopped her.

"Even though I'm so attracted to you, I was hesitant. That must have sent mixed messages and made it more difficult for you."

"You said the problem was that I called you Antony."

"That was true, but there was more. I'd like the chance to do better," he said.

This was a new approach. No dinner, no drinks, no green silk dress. Or, perhaps, he didn't mean tonight. "Soon?" Minnie asked, her voice going squeaky.

"Within the hour, if possible."

It seemed too quick, even cold. But wasn't this the modern way to discuss things? Lay it all out. Get to the bottom line.

"Have I shocked you?" Ronald asked.

"No, I just needed a moment. I guess we could try again."

Ronald started the car. Minnie took a deep breath and made an inventory of her underthings. Not fabulous but satisfactory.

He hummed as they drove onto Estero Shores Drive. He parked in the garage, and, when he helped her out of the car, he kissed her forehead. Gripping his forearm as she rose from the seat, she could feel a ribbon of tense muscle.

Though he had seemed almost lazy earlier, he was now strung so tightly that he seemed to bounce as he walked. While waiting for the elevator he whistled tunelessly under his breath. He walked so briskly down the concrete walkway to his condo that she could barely keep up.

Once inside he asked if she would like a drink. His tone said that he really didn't want to take the time.

Minnie sensed that she had some catching up to do. "Yes. Whiskey and water."

He poured two generous drinks and led her out to the patio. They sank into plush chairs, feet up. Minnie took a couple of healthy drinks from her glass, noticing that Ronald took the merest of sips.

They exchanged smiles; there seemed to be nothing to talk about. Again, he hummed from time to time.

After a few minutes Ronald rose and bent over her. He put one hand behind her head and kissed her on the lips. There was strength and urgency this time. "I'll just go in. Please come whenever you're ready."

What was he doing, leaving her alone when her resolve was weakening? This whole proposition felt like a set-up instead of a romantic encounter. Minnie argued with herself: should she just be a grown up and admit that she would enjoy some sex, or should she be a baby and go home. What would she do if she left? Walk to her place, shower, read.

Saxophone-heavy music drifted from the bedroom. She took another deep swallow of whiskey.

As she moved through the living room she began to unbutton her blouse. Her breasts seemed not over-large, but voluptuous in the shadowy room. She entered the bedroom. The only light, a silvery white that came through the fabric at the window, painted Ronald's head and shoulders as he lay in bed. He came up on one elbow as she moved closer, removing her clothes. She slid in beside him, the quilt enveloping them. When Minnie's head went sideways toward the pillow she had a moment of whiskey-inspired vertigo, but she settled onto the satin and Ronald pulled her close. He held her head back by her hair and kissed her neck, then his full, warm lips moved slowly downward to her breasts. As soon as her arms went around him and their bodies pressed together, she realized this would not be anything like last time. He became engrossed in pleasing her, and she was grateful for her own response.

When she ran an arm down his back, her fingers came upon some fabric. She traced over it with her fingertips. No, it couldn't be. It felt like the back of a bra. Dumbfounded, she fingered the fasteners. All sexual energy left her body, but Ronald didn't seem to notice. He was fully intent on matters at hand, and Minnie realized he would not be easily distracted. Feeling devilish now, she slipped her thumb beneath the elastic and pulled the strap away from his body. Then she let it snap back.

Ronald's body went perfectly still and he groaned in embarrassment. Minnie gripped the edge of the quilt and threw it back, exposing them both to the knees. Just visible in the wan light was more fabric on his hips. Matching panties. The front of the bra wasn't molded like a woman's, but was simply a flat strip of black lace.

"What's this?" she asked.

Ronald was suddenly a flurry of activity, tearing the two pieces from himself and throwing them on the floor. "Oh, God. It's nothing, Minnie; it means nothing. It just helps me enjoy sex. Please don't be put off." Now naked, he stared into her face, trying to read her reaction, his own face ghostly white.

Minnie sat straight up to avoid his gaze. Thinking back on the evening, on Ronald's early quietness followed by his odd behavior, she probably should have guessed that something was off. But, even with a clearer warning, nothing like this would have come to mind. She'd read Anne Landers often enough to know that these behaviors are fairly common and do not indicate perversity. Nevertheless, she would not be able to look at him as a sexual partner again.

"I'm sorry, but it does put me off," she said, looking at him.

As he searched her face for compassion, she saw confusion and guilt in his eyes. What a terrible burden, she thought. What kind of compulsion would require a man to take such a chance, to subject himself to scorn?

She scooted down again, replacing the quilt so that they were both covered. He turned flat on his back, staring upward and reached for her hand.

"Ronald, this is impossible for me. But I really don't think less of you."

"Are you sure? I couldn't stand it if you were laughing at me."

"I'm not laughing. You must have met women who are okay with this."

"A few. But I didn't like any of them as well as I like you."

She pressed his hand. "The right one will come along," she said. Marge Higgins came to mind, and Minnie chastised herself. One mean corner of her mind *was* laughing at Ronald—at Ronald *and* Marge—and he, at least, deserved better.

"Couldn't you have prepared me somehow?" she asked.

"Can you think of a way?"

Minnie tried to conjure up a conversation that might incorporate such news. "I guess you're right."

"I hoped that the passion would carry you beyond it." His voice had been crippled along with his pride.

"Thank you for trusting me that much," she said.

He rolled onto his side, ducking his face from her sight, and pressed her curled fingers to his forehead. Though he couldn't speak, Minnie felt everything being transmitted through that touch: shame, fear, contrition and emotions she couldn't name but could feel in his trembling grip.

When she stroked the top of his head with her free hand there was a great sigh, and his body sank into the bed as if that terrible secret had kept it hovering.

22

The nearer Detective Wilkins came to Catherine's address the further his heart sank. He knew this neighborhood. He had knocked on more than a few of its doors searching for young men in trouble. A mother or sister would invariably answer. He would look directly into their faces and see practiced lies circling behind the eyes. He often sensed these women weighing their chances: Who should they fear more, the detective on the doorstep or the brother or husband in the back room?

Wilkins drove by the house slowly, taking in details. It was small, its fenced lawn neater than most, but a coat of paint could not erase sixty-odd years of neglect. One shoulder of the roof stooped with age, sending the eye to the neighbor's yard where two cars sat propped on bricks. The door of one vehicle hung open, exposing ratty upholstery. If Catherine was united with Mike in a scheme to provide her with hefty commissions, the result of those efforts was not evident. This gave Wilkins

Minnie And The Manatees

hope. He made a U-turn at the intersection and parked his pickup across the street, a half-block away from the house.

A mid-nineties Lexus passed him and pulled into Catherine's driveway. A man, maybe five-ten, approached her front door. Wilkins noted that his movements were constrained, as if bulk or muscles pulled against the fabric of his shirt and pants. As the man put a key in the lock and entered without the need for an invitation, Wilkins let out a huff of resignation. He drove slowly past the house again, noting the license number of the Lexus.

First thing the next morning the detective's spirits were lifted when he picked up his phone and heard, "This is Catherine James, from Estero Shores."

"I remember you, Catherine."

"I have a favor to ask."

"Ask away."

"I live in a rather disreputable part of town, and it has become a habit of mine to watch the street closely. Last night when I was waiting for a friend to arrive, I noticed a large black truck go slowly by the house, turn around, and park down the street."

Detective Wilkins put his hand over the mouthpiece to hide a clearing of his throat. He glanced across the two abutting desks to where an Hispanic detective typed his notes. Then he hunched over the receiver to muffle his voice.

"Did you feel threatened by that?"

"Uncomfortable. As soon as my friend arrived the truck left. It seemed too much of a coincidence."

Wilkins could not think of a reply, and Catherine continued, "Can you check it out? I caught part of the license number."

Wilkins pretended to listen to the familiar identification.

"I'll drop by the sales office later if that's convenient," he said.

"I'll be there. Thanks."

Returning to his work, Wilkins learned some disturbing facts. The Lexus which had pulled into Catherine's driveway was registered to Mike McCreary whose address was in Naples, and his upscale residential property was owned by Mike and Janice McCreary. After a dispiriting half-hour of computer research, he shoved back from his desk on his rolling chair and clapped his hands on his thighs. He rose and paced a few feet beside his desk, then walked outside.

Breathing deeply of the morning air, which still held a hint of freshness, he moved down the street. He rolled his shirt sleeves then rubbed his face with both hands. At the corner convenience store he bought a cold can of Dr. Pepper. Stepping back outside he drank quickly, eager for the jolt of caffeine to prop up his deteriorating mood.

The large and troubled McCreary family was familiar to law enforcement officers in south Florida. Members of two generations were regularly in jail for theft or brawling or drunkenness. But there was no history of major felonies and certainly nothing so ugly as murder. Had that line now been crossed? Wilkins tossed the empty can into a dumpster which poked out of an alley. How closely was Catherine tied to this disturbed family?

Catherine was with clients when Wilkins arrived, so he stood aside, waiting. She wore a pink suit with pink and black pumps, distracting Wilkins from the model of the development spread across a table. She handled an older couple with cheerful confidence, and he could see why people would want her to sell their properties. The man and woman left, smiling, their heads poked together, studying a slick brochure.

"Hello, Detective," she said, turning to him. "Thank you for coming."

"Can we go to your office?" he asked.

A frown creased Catherine's forehead. "Is it bad news?"

"Just private," he said.

They sat as they had the previous time, in opposing chairs. Wilkins cleared his throat, swallowed, and tried a smile which failed him. On the drive over he had changed his story a half-dozen times, arguing with himself about how much to divulge. Now, so close to her and feeling that strong attraction again, he decided the least said the better. He could not mention McCreary because that would betray Mrs. Zuccarelli, and, equally important to him at the moment, he did not wish to put himself in a poorer light than necessary.

"I have a rather embarrassing admission to make." He licked his dry lips. "That was me in the truck last night."

Catherine tilted her head.

"When I interviewed you I found you so . . . attractive." He blushed; he had almost said, beguiling. "This can be no surprise. It must happen all the time."

She merely righted her head with no change in her facial expression, and he felt heat rising in his cheeks.

"My curiosity overcame my good sense. Instead of simply asking you for a date, I found out where you lived. Last night I was going to stop in and visit, got cold feet, and parked. When your visitor came, I took off."

He licked his lips again. "Have you got a soda or something?"

Catherine disappeared down a hallway and came back with a bottle of cold water. She handed it to him, studying his face.

She didn't return to her chair, but stood. "Is that all, then?" she asked.

He nodded as he twisted the bottle cap. "I promise. And now I've spoiled my chance to ask you out."

"Yes," she said. "I'm not in the phone book, so you went to some trouble to find out where I live. It must be, at the very least, an indiscretion to use your position as a police officer to check up on someone for personal reasons."

"It was poor judgment. I apologize."

"So I won't see your black truck cruising my street again?"

Wilkins was shaking his head as she moved out of her office. He followed her, heard the tinkling of the bell as she opened the outer door, then found himself standing in the afternoon sun, the water bottle in one hand and its cap in the other.

Embarrassed, he drove off, wondering why a woman like that would live where she did. Even without McCreary's help, her talent would earn her enough money to do better. Perhaps it was a ruse.

23

Minnie and Ronald sat thigh-to-thigh on a metal seat, skimming the Everglades on what seemed to be a flat piece of tin strapped to a jet engine. The pilot sped toward the shore, then just as one was sure they would land among the sawgrass, he swung the boat sideways, putting them into a skidding turn.

Clamping one hand over her mouth to avoid screaming, Minnie gripped Ronald's arm with the other. She had anticipated a gentle cruise to observe alligators, but this was more like one of Disney's rides. There were seven passengers in all, and the young boy sitting behind Minnie yelled with delight.

After another five minutes of this, the pilot idled the boat to give them some local history. As he explained about tannin staining the water, an alligator slithered up alongside, right next to Minnie. His tail trailed along the length of the boat. The lip of the craft rose only twelve inches off the surface of the water, and she sat closer than that to the edge. He was close enough that she could have touched his head without even leaning over. Sweat broke out under her arms, but no one else seemed concerned. Then his bulging eyes rolled upward and met her own. She let out a squeal and almost shoved Ronald off the seat trying to move away. Suddenly the pilot jumped from his raised seat at the back of the boat and lodged one of his legs between her and the elongated head.

"These guys can leap sideways," he said.

This activity must have annoyed the alligator because he sank slowly, the water creeping over his flat nose, then his eyes, then his six-foot body. The pilot climbed back to his seat and they moved off.

Minnie was still disconcerted as they walked to the car. "Do you think that alligator might actually have jumped sideways like the pilot said, or was that a Chamber of Commerce thing?" she asked Ronald.

"I don't know if he was serious, but it makes a darn good story. He sure did move fast once he noticed what was going on."

Minnie found her reflection in the window of the car and ran fingers through her hair in an attempt to put it back in place.

"It will take more than that," Ronald said, teasing.

He opened her door and she slid inside. They rolled over the gravel parking area and bumped onto the narrow highway. With a long drive ahead, she settled into the corner hoping to doze. She decided this was nice, this relationship unfettered by emotion. Ronald was such a decent man, yet maybe destined to be lonely. He would need to find a very open-minded woman, or someone so much in love that she could overcome her hesitation.

The morning after her shocking discovery and Ronald's humiliation, she had found a note stuck under her door.

Minnie, thank you for being so understanding. I could easily have been destroyed. Your kindness allows me to hope that we might still be friends. I am forever indebted. Ronald

Since then they had enjoyed an afternoon at the beach and, a few days later, a play. Their friendship had deepened because of the experience.

When she got home after their dinner of hamburgers and beer, Minnie notice that her cell phone display area held a message. "One missed call." Oh, dear, she thought, having had mixed success in retrieving them. Slipping on her glasses, she studied the innumerable buttons on the small unit and decided on Options. *Call that Number?* Not necessarily. Option number two was, *Check Time?* No. She pulled the instruction booklet from the kitchen drawer. *Press the Multi-*

use/Message button and dial the Voice Mail number and your personal PIN.

After a few moments, and with a sense of victory, she heard the recorded voice of Detective Wilkins; he wanted her to call him at his home in the evening if necessary. That sounded ominous. She dialed the number wondering what he wanted to question her about now.

"Hello Mrs. Zuccarelli," he said, startling Minnie for a moment until she realized he must have a caller ID service. "I've got some good news."

"That's a relief."

"The police in Ft. Lauderdale located some of Mrs. Logan's jewelry at a pawn shop, and they have the man in custody."

Minnie didn't see where the good news came in.

"He doesn't speak a word of English."

"Oh." It started to come together. "So he couldn't have threatened me on the phone? What if he had someone else do it?"

"He's a fall guy from Miami, a minion in an organized gang that moves around the state. Someone higher up gave him the lead on Mrs. Logan. From what we can gather, they have a front man who identifies victims by hanging around high-end jewelry stores. I just don't see any possible connection between whoever that might be and your community . . . how that person could possibly have known about you seeing the thief running away."

"What does this mean?"

"Most important, I don't think you are in any danger. But you will have to decide which of your acquaintances wanted to frighten you. Try to remember who, exactly, was around when you told the story and who those people might have passed it on to. The other good news is that we won't be bugging your line any longer. Would you like to keep the cell phone as a thank-you?"

"I don't need it."

"Then I'll pick it up some time if you promise me a cup of coffee."

"Just give me a little notice." Minnie almost clicked the End button, then said, "Wait. Did he kill Mrs. Logan?"

"His story is that she fought with him, he pushed her and she fell. Her head caught the corner of the bed frame. It fits what we found at the scene."

Minnie had been sitting on the arm of the sofa. She let herself fall backward onto its cushions, her knees wrapped over the edge, with her feet dangling. For a minute she thought about poor Mrs. Logan's struggle, then remembered the trauma she had experienced because of the resultant phone call. It was sickening to think that someone she knew had created all that fear. Minnie recalled that in the pool the morning after the robbery Marge had been especially irritating. Something about Ronald. Marge was a piece of work, but would she be capable of this kind of

Minnie And The Manatees

cruelty? And the voice. Could Marge disguise hers that well?

Minnie rolled to her side, then sat up. "Mind your own damn business," she said in her best baritone. It sounded like a woman trying to be a man. She tried it again, pulling the sound from deep in her lungs and adding an accent. "Mind your own damn business." That one wasn't half bad. She guessed that with a bit of practice she might be able to pull it off. Encouraged, she drew herself up, took a deep breath and gave it her all. Pretty good.

She dialed Antony's number and, when he answered she said, "Mind your own damn business."

"What the hell?" Antony shouted.

"Hey, it's Minnie. Did that sound like a man?"

"Yes it did," he stammered. "What are you up to?"

"I just spoke with Detective Wilkins." She relayed the news about the thief's capture. "I was wondering if our dear friend Marge Higgins could have made the call to me."

"I wouldn't put it past her, but how would you prove it?"

"I think I have one possible connection."

When Minnie stretched to wakefulness the next morning, it was eight-thirty. "Cripes," she said, frustrated that she didn't have time to wash and dry her hair. After setting up the coffee, she brushed her teeth, had a three minute shower and slipped a caftan over her head. It fell to her toes as Ronald knocked on her door.

Scuffing into slippers she went to greet him.

"Am I early?" he asked, assessing her.

"No. I'm late. Come on in. You'll just have to put up with this old face with no makeup."

"I can come back."

"Surely I don't look *that* bad."

Ronald laughed. "You look fine. I was just trying to be helpful."

"That's one of your finest points, and, in fact, that's why I asked you to come over. To be helpful."

Ronald sat on a bar stool, leaning on the counter. "What do you need, drain unclogging? Battery charging?"

"A little detective work," Minnie said, sitting beside him. "You said I could always count on you."

He nodded. "Of course."

"Let me give you a real short version of something that troubles me. Some time ago I received a threatening phone call. It sounded like a man."

"Did you go to the police?"

"Yes. It has all been taken care of. But now I believe the call was made by a woman disguising her voice."

"What was it about, Minnie?"

"It's too long a story for now. I want to get to the favor I'm asking. How well do you know Marge Higgins?"

"We say hello, pass the time of day."

"She really dislikes me, and I'm pretty sure she's the person who made that call."

"That's pretty drastic; why would she do that?"

"She and I and Antony go back a long way and I'd rather not go into the details. Do you mind?"

"It's your business. But what can I do?"

"Have you ever considered going out with her?"

"Not since my first date with you."

Minnie stroked his arm to convey her appreciation. "I don't know how else to get close enough to her to learn the truth. I'm asking you to get to know her. She's such a bragging, talkative creature, I think she might confess to someone who gained her confidence."

Ronald shifted his weight on the stool. "If she did it, would you confront her?"

"No, she would never have to know about our collusion. I just want to be sure who it was so I can get it out of my mind."

Ronald walked into the kitchen and poured two cups of coffee. He added a spoonful of sugar and some milk to hers and passed it across the counter. "This isn't my kind of thing, Minnie, but if it's important to you I'll give it a try."

24

Minnie finished her eleven o'clock client just as Catherine entered the shop for her lunch-hour appointment. As Catherine settled into place, Minnie noticed puffiness around Catherine's eyes. Her makeup was obvious, as though she had applied more than usual. She was quiet, and Minnie usually honored her clients' moods, but she was sure Catherine would want to know about the police finding the man who robbed Mrs. Logan. She dropped her voice to a whisper as she relayed the details. She thought this would be wonderful news, but Catherine didn't say anything. Minnie leaned closer, "But you see, your suspicions about Mike were all wrong."

Catherine said, "That's a relief, I guess. But I was stupid to think it in the first place." Then she sat quiet, again.

Minnie removed the old polish from Catherine's nails, but the silence was too much. Finally, Minnie could no longer ignore her friend's odd behavior. "You getting enough sleep?" she asked, keeping her voice beneath the hum of the shop. "Is Mike away again?"

"As a matter of fact, yes. He took Adrian to Disney World for three days for his birthday."

Minnie assumed Mike's wife was part of the celebration, which would account for Catherine's appearance and her depression.

"Antony and I went there for a full week not long after it opened. I can still see the joy and wonder on all those young faces."

"You would have been a great mother, Minnie," Catherine said.

"Maybe. I'm sure it's a tougher job than it looks."

"You know that detective Wilkins?" Catherine asked.

"Sure." Minnie glanced up, raising her eyebrows.

"Is he married?" Catherine asked.

"I don't think so. He told me once about an engagement that went wrong."

"One night he drove by my place, parked, and actually watched until Mike arrived."

Minnie kept her eyes on her work, but had to swallow. This is what had come of her admission to Detective Wilkins that she suspected Mike. "Why on earth would he do that?"

"He said he was in my neighborhood simply because he's attracted to me, but even that makes me uncomfortable."

"He no doubt has a crush on you. Besides, in your neighborhood, having a cop around is a good thing. If you don't mind my asking, why do you stay there?"

"That area used to be a pretty decent neighborhood. It's the same house where I grew up."

"Still, you know it could mean trouble at some point, you being on your own."

"Something keeps me there. I sometimes think I'm still that little girl waiting for her folks to come home. Isn't that silly? As if they would show up if only I waited long enough."

"You were alone a lot as a kid?"

"Almost every day and night. My folks both worked, and then partied. My strongest memory is waiting for the front door to open."

"And, they're no longer with us?" Minnie asked, looking into Catherine's face.

"One night, when I was seventeen, they partied too much and didn't make it home."

"That must have been terrible for you."

"It was a long time ago. Far too long for me to still cling to that old house. I probably need a good shrink."

"What you need is some real security, and I can't help feeling Mike isn't able to give you that."

"I shouldn't need to get it from someone else."

"That sounds really good on all the talk shows, but I think it seldom works. Nature has programmed us to depend on a mate for emotional support and ninety-nine percent of us can't break the pattern."

"If you're right, I'd have to break it off with Mike, because that part of our relationship is not going to change."

As Minnie's hands worked automatically, she looked into Catherine's sad eyes. "I didn't mean to suggest that."

Catherine nodded. "I know, Minnie. You have only put words to my thoughts. I need to face the fact that he and I are going nowhere."

Catherine stayed up late anticipating that Mike would call as soon as they got back from Disney World. At five o'clock in the morning she got up and sat at her dinette table, too dispirited to even make coffee. Catherine knew that part of the reason she stayed with Mike was to avoid being alone. But Minnie was alone; millions of women were alone at this very moment. Some of them were probably sitting at their kitchen tables at five a.m. Maybe the day ahead loomed long and maybe the evenings were worse, but they were brave enough not to settle. Surely she could find that kind of courage.

Feeling strengthened by resolve, she moved to the shower and missed Mike's call. She played his message back twice, listening to his voice. For all its warmth, it might have been a call to a business acquaintance. He wanted to meet for breakfast. Nothing about not calling last night. Nothing about missing her.

He was waiting outside the restaurant and grinned as she approached. "Hi beautiful," he said, holding her shoulders and kissing her on the cheek. "I always forget how gorgeous you are. I missed you."

Catherine led him inside. On the way to their table Mike grabbed a newspaper from an empty chair. Once seated, Catherine saw that it was yesterday's paper, recognizing the headline about NASA's cash problem and the possibility of privatization of the program. Those kinds of rumors had circulated regularly for a few years. There was speculation that the entire shuttle operation might become private, the astronauts, flight directors and controllers becoming employees of an independent shuttle management company.

Her instinct was to ask Mike whether this possibility dismayed him as it did her, but he was concentrating on the menu. Catherine remembered when the two of them had attended a lift-off. Their love was fresh then, when heightened emotions magnified every sensation. At the moment of separation, as the aircraft swept away from the massive rocket that had thrust it beyond earth's gravity, they gripped each other's hands as if sharing the elation of the crew.

Now, studying him while he ignored her, she pondered how far they had come from those electric days. Their love had changed, as most loves do, to a less charged relationship. And she

Minnie And The Manatees

did remember a time when she was not bothered by doubts. But recently a veil had settled between them through which she saw and felt everything vaguely. The flashes of silent communication were gone, the bright moments dulled. He seemed older to her ever since the day she'd changed the lock on her door; she had watched him shrink at that moment standing on her doorstep, and he had never regained his ground.

When thinking clearly she couldn't imagine him being involved in the deaths at Estero Shores, but the fact that she had even considered the possibility made her realize how badly her confidence in him had eroded. Whenever she recalled Mike's many absences, she wondered whether he had told her the truth about his travels. And no matter what they discussed, even if it was something trivial, part of her mind listened while another part scrutinized every nuance.

"So Adrian had a good time on his birthday trip?" she asked.

Mike put his menu aside. "Terrific. He especially liked the rides. I'm having huevos rancheros. What about you?"

"Oatmeal and toast."

Catherine took a deep breath. "Mike . . ." She was ready to say, *I was really lonely when you were away,* but it came out with more honesty. "I am really lonely."

He wrapped his hand around hers. "Cat, you know I wish things were different. I'd have loved to have you along."

"Except that Adrian can never know about me. I can never share the biggest part of your life. Will anything ever change?"

Mike looked around. "Cat, not here for God's sake."

"It's as good a place as any," Catherine said, withdrawing her hand from his. She picked up her handbag and rose. "I need more than you can give me, Mike."

In the parking lot he caught up to her, grabbed her arm and spun her around. "What is the matter?" he demanded.

"Aside from the fact that I'm excluded from your life?" Catherine stopped herself before she could spit out the rest of her thought. Could she say it and destroy everything? Then the words came out. "I don't know if I trust you anymore."

His face fell. He blinked twice, as though not only his hearing must be impaired, but his eyesight as well. "This is sudden."

"Not really."

He looked at her intently, studying her face. "So, you've given it a lot of thought?"

Catherine couldn't speak, but nodded, then looked down at her feet.

She could hear Mike's breathing.

"Cat, you don't mean it," he said. "Say you don't mean it."

She stayed motionless.

"There's someone else, is that it? Why can't you just be honest."

She looked into his face. "No, Mike. No one else. Just us. And that's the problem. It will always be just us. I live in a secret place, and it's too lonely."

"I love you, Cat."

"Maybe you do, but it's not enough. I'm sorry."

He reached out as if to touch her, then changed his mind. His hand dropped to his side. Finally he spoke, "I can't blame you, Cat."

He didn't look back, his sturdy legs carrying him to the restaurant.

Catherine stared after him, hardly comprehending. Even though they had both said their goodbyes, it still seemed impossible that he could leave her standing alone in the parking lot. She put one hand to her forehead to rub away a flash of memory—an empty house, a watched door through which her parents would never emerge. That same shock of pure loneliness made her stumble as she moved to her car.

Miserable with uncertainty, she sat for several minutes debating whether to go back inside. But returning to Mike now would, forever, destroy her credibility. He would feel free to treat her in any way that suited him. And, having once been defeated by her own weakness, she would feel trapped.

Catherine pulled out of the parking lot. As she glanced over her shoulder to check oncoming traffic, she saw a black pickup parked on the street with the driver sitting inside. Detective Wilkins? She stepped on her brake, trying to see through the windshield of the truck. But the car behind her honked, forcing her to keep moving. As she pulled away, she checked her rear-view mirror and was relieved when the truck did not follow.

25

When Catherine James stumbled and almost fell against her car, Detective Wilkins grabbed the door handle of his truck, ready to leap out and run to her assistance. But she gathered herself, opened her car door and slid into the scat. While he watched her sitting in her car for a few minutes, Wilkins dissected what he had just witnessed.

When Mike McCreary turned on his heels and walked away from Catherine, Wilkins felt encouraged for the first time in days. Parked on the street, he couldn't hear what had been said in the parking lot but it was definitely an argument. A low-keyed one, perhaps, but he crossed his fingers that it was a serious one. Maybe Catherine was free of McCreary; maybe she could get away in time, for Mike McCreary's own freedom might well be coming to an end.

While checking up on McCreary for his own purposes, Wilkins had mentioned his name around the precinct and learned that he was a minor suspect in a drug operation under surveillance. There was no solid evidence against him, only hints from the most unreliable of sources—snitches who would say anything for a twenty dollar bill. The detectives working the drug case thought he was probably involved but did not consider him a key figure. Though McCreary was not on their short list, they had questioned him about his whereabouts on two different occasions in the last few months. Janice McCreary had supplied him with alibis. In the opinion of the detectives, Janice's testimony, if it came to that, should not carry much more credibility than that of the snitches. But, they told Wilkins, she was an attractive woman who presented herself well, and she might convince a jury. But Wilkins knew that, alibis or not, the walls were closing in around McCreary.

When Catherine started her car and exited the lot, Wilkins was startled because she looked right at his front windshield. He was relieved when she drove off. He could imagine how angry she would be if she thought he was trailing her instead of her boyfriend.

Waiting for McCreary to re-emerge from the restaurant, Wilkins fought off drowsiness. He pulled his key from the ignition and tapped the heavy key ring rhythmically against the steering post. Then he stroked the rabbit's foot that dangled from the steel hoop. He hadn't slept well since his return from Orlando and wished he had never taken the trip.

Minnie And The Manatees

With a couple of days off and nothing on his mind but trying to solve the puzzle of Catherine James's attachment to McCreary, Wilkins had followed Mike, Janice and a young man, mile-by-mile, all the way to Orlando. When he realized their destination was Disney World, he was disgusted at the waste of his time and checked into their same hotel for the night.

While eating a solitary breakfast in the hotel restaurant the next morning, he glanced out to the lobby and saw Mike talking to a man whose face was somewhat familiar. He knew the name would not come to him. It was just the face. Maybe a mug shot, maybe one of the hundreds of men who had been processed in the precinct in the last while. Without staring, he memorized what he could: pale skin and eyes, straw-colored hair, sharp cheekbones, dressed well. Taller than Mike, he stood slightly slump-shouldered as they conversed head-to-head. Then the man clapped Mike on the shoulder and walked off.

The elevator doors opened, and Janice and the boy emerged. In describing Janice, his fellow officers had not done her justice. Tall and thin, with red hair pulled into a gleaming knot, she walked boldly, a woman accustomed to commanding attention. The boy dragged behind a bit, looking around the lobby. Then, spotting Mike, his eyes lit up. He ran to Mike's side and took his hand. Mike wrapped his other arm around the boy and gave him a rough-house hug. As the boy broke from the embrace, smiling, Wilkins recognized his Down Syndrome appearance.

Wilkins moaned inwardly and pushed his half-finished plate of bacon and eggs away. He had just witnessed expressions of total love between a man and his son, and Wilkins' own actions, or those of his cohorts, could blast that happiness into oblivion. He motioned the waitress for his check and left the McCreary family to their weekend pleasures.

As Wilkins relived that disturbing scene, he saw Mike McCreary exit the restaurant. McCreary looked to where Catherine's car had been parked, then he got into the Lexus. Wilkins followed as McCreary drove directly to the highway and headed south toward Naples. When McCreary pulled off at the exit which would take him to his home, Wilkins turned around. Nothing very interesting was likely to happen if he was headed there, and Mike would be easy to pick up again.

Wilkins sat at his desk, undecided about how to proceed, if at all. He had learned from nosing around that the pale guy in the hotel lobby in Orlando was named Garrett, a petty dealer, one of those people the cops kept an eye on while looking for bigger fish. Putting him and McCreary together might draw McCreary deeper into the ongoing drug investigation. That case was not his responsibility. He admitted he would like to have the man out of the way, both to protect Catherine

Minnie And The Manatees

and to get closer to her. But if McCreary was not a major suspect, and if she truly loved him, did he want to be responsible for hurting her? And what of the boy? Was there someone to support him if Mike landed in jail? The extended McCreary family, whose mottled histories were public record, did not seem to qualify.

Perhaps he could resolve one part of the quandary by visiting Catherine. Maybe he could find out whether or not the argument he had watched meant she was through with Mike.

He entered the Estero Shores outer office, causing the silly bell to clang. While pretending interest in the pin-spotted map on the wall, he waited for Catherine to come out of her office. When she didn't, he approached her door. Then he heard her coming from another direction, down the hallway, and turned toward her. Her eyes were ringed in pink.

"Oh, Detective," she said, stuffing a Kleenex into the pocket of her blazer. "I didn't realize anyone was here. Doing some more snooping?" She raised her chin bravely, but the corners of her mouth remained drawn down.

"Hello, Ms. James. Or can I call you Catherine?"

"Sure, since you already know so much about me. Go on in," she said.

He entered her office and stood while she went around behind her desk and sat down. "More questions?" she asked.

"I know you're angry with me for tracking you down. I would really like an opportunity to apologize in a more private setting. Would you agree to having dinner with me?"

"What?"

"Dinner. A date, sort of. I'd really like to get to know you better."

"I thought I told you I was involved with someone."

"Things change. I was hoping." He tried a smile and pulled his key ring from a pocket, dangling it. "I even brought my rabbit's foot for luck."

She looked up at him for several seconds with no expression. He returned the key ring to his pocket.

"Are you married?" she asked.

Wilkins sat down. "No. Where did you get that idea?"

"It comes to mind. Children?"

"None."

She bit her bottom lip and turned her face to the wall. Then she stood up abruptly. "Excuse me a minute," she said, going out of the office and back down the hallway.

She might have been close to tears, Wilkins thought. The decent thing to do was to leave, but she hadn't given him a definite no, yet. Naturally curious, his eyes ranged over her desk. Her appointment book was lying open with a slash of pink highlighter marking an entry. Listening for her, and arching to look more closely, he

Minnie And The Manatees

read "Mike-Tampa-3." The date was two and a half months prior. He went to the doorway and glanced down the hall. He heard a muffled sound of her blowing her nose, probably coming from the restroom. He returned to her desk and flipped to the next week in the appointment book. Once again an entry was slashed through with the pink highlighter. "Mike-Atlanta-2."

Hearing a toilet flush, he sat back down.

Catherine called to him from down the hall. "Detective, why don't you check with me next week." A door closed.

Several possibilities bothered Wilkins as he drove off. There were other notes on the calendar on those days, indicating she had been at work and not off on short vacations with Mike. Could she be involved in Mike's business and those notes be some kind of code? Or, she was keeping tabs on him for some other purpose. The only thing he could be sure of was that his buddies at the station would love to have a look at that book.

26

When Catherine accepted a date for dinner the next week, Wilkins forgot everything except the pleasure of being alone with her. He was disappointed when she insisted on taking her own car and meeting him, but it was a first step. He had suggested The Bridge for their dinner, but Catherine said she would prefer something very casual. They settled on a crab house with plywood tables covered in vinyl, which offered a choice of tap beer or wine. Catherine wore little makeup, jeans and sneakers. If not for the worry lines in her forehead, she could have been a teenager.

Wilkins hadn't dated anyone he really cared about for a while and found the going rough. Because he was so grateful she had agreed to the date, and since he had some ground to make up, he measured every word before it came out of his mouth. Consequently, conversation died early. They were both eating at a rapid pace and smiling falsely across the table.

"This isn't working out so well, detective," Catherine said, putting her crushed paper napkin on her plate. "Not your fault. I'm poor company lately."

"You know what might help?" he said. "You could call me Dave instead of detective."

Catherine actually smiled. "Dave. Yes, that might help. I do tend to think of you as an interrogator."

"Why don't *you* ask the questions then?"

"Okay." She leaned toward him. "Tell me, Dave, how long have you been on the police force?"

She played a television host, asking things like, are you a Florida native, where did you go to school. It became silly enough that at one point they laughed. The sudden happiness in her face stunned him.

"Gosh, you're beautiful," he said.

"That's off the topic, Dave. That kind of diversion will get us nowhere."

"How about, gosh, I enjoy being with you."

"Better." For the first time there was a softness in her eyes, as if she was seeing beyond his badge. Their eyes held for a few moments before she broke off and poured the last of her beer into the glass. There was less than an ounce left, so she pushed it aside.

"I should be going."

He wanted to beg for a little more time, but knew he should be satisfied to have shared dinner. "I'm going to follow you home," he said.

"I'm not a baby."

"You forget, I know where you live."

Her face dropped; she was not pleased at the remark. "It's your gas," she said.

Catherine punched the remote to open the garage door. The interior light came on and she pulled inside, then turned in her seat to see the detective's truck stop at the curb. She lowered the door and entered the house, clicking on several lights. After a few minutes she saw that he had driven off.

Tossing her tennis shoes into the closet she decided that the experimental date had gone as well as could be expected, given that she had spent no amount of time with any man but Mike for years. Even though he was a detective, Wilkins didn't convey the sense of physical security she felt with Mike. But then, Dave was much younger, and newly smitten. Even Mike had been awkward in the beginning.

As she poured herself a glass of wine, the phone rang.

"Hi, Cat."

She didn't reply.

"Please don't hang up. I won't be long."

Catherine steeled herself. After more than a week of continuous tears, she had decided she could survive without Mike and all his lies.

"Do you know that guy you went out with is a cop?"

Minnie And The Manatees

There was no point in asking how long he had been watching her. "I didn't notice your car."

"I'm in Janice's."

"Well, actually, he's a detective. And rather nice."

"He's just using you, Cat. To get to me."

Catherine slammed the receiver into its cradle, hoping she had burst his ear drum.

She downed the wine, showered and furiously scrubbed her hair, moving as fast as possible to vent her anger. It was not until she was seated in bed with the newspaper on her lap that the full meaning of his comment struck her.

Mike had once given her his home number to use in case of an emergency. Hoping Janice would answer and Mike would be exposed, she dialed.

"Yup," Mike said after just one ring.

"It's Catherine."

"Cat, I'm glad you called back. What I said came out wrong. I sure didn't mean that any man wouldn't want you just for yourself."

"Why did you say the detective was trying to get to you?"

"They've been nosing around lately. I don't know what's got them sniffing my way. I just thought that, since I had nothing to give them, they might try another angle."

"Well, this feels real comfortable, being included in a police investigation. What the hell is going on, Mike?"

"It's nothing, Cat. You don't need to be embroiled in my family matters. The less you know the better."

"So the detective won't be able to drag information from me? Mike, this is disgusting and just proves I've made the right decision about you."

"I deserve it, Cat. I accept it. Just don't make the wrong one about the cop."

27

Minnie hadn't felt so tense for a long time as she did while waiting for Antony. She had not seen him since their lunch when she told him about dating Ronald. They had talked on the phone about superficialities, avoiding anything personal. But today was a day she could share with no one else; the sanctuary had called to say Helena had been moved to the viewing tank.

She took a deep breath and opened the door to his knock.

His handsome grin had been replaced by a smile, almost pathetic in its hopefulness. He hesitated, then stepped inside and gave her a light hug. "Good to see you," he said. She'd never before felt such stiffness in his body. She wanted to say, don't try so hard, don't hurt so much. But she also wanted to hug him tighter. She had missed him, too, and spent long hours wondering what he could ever do to convince her of his loyalty. Was there any way to get past his deception?

She fussed with her purse, checking her wallet and keys, then went looking for her sunglasses. When she re-emerged from the bedroom he was standing outside on the landing.

"Super day," he said. "I'm glad you called."

The drive seemed to take forever and no matter what they talked about she heard him asking, *are you still seeing that man?* But he didn't actually ask, and she didn't offer.

An iron railing ringed the huge tank that held Helena. Two other manatees swam on the opposite side from where she floated, snugged up to the metal wall. Minnie stretched her upper body for a better view. If it were possible for a manatee to express hopelessness, Minnie thought she was looking at it.

The other manatees rolled and jostled each other, but one remained motionless, her eyes closed. That had to be Helena.

"She's not moving at all," Minnie murmured.

A young, female attendant was standing nearby, and explained, "She's unfamiliar with this tank, and she's tired. We think she is over thirty years old, and the operation took a toll."

"I can't see what you've done," Minnie said.

"When she moves you'll see that we had to remove most of her right flipper. She always turns to the right now; she can't propel herself in the other direction."

"Does that mean she'll never be able to return to the wild?" Minnie asked.

"Not necessarily. We'll monitor her closely and see how she manages."

The young woman left them, calling back over her shoulder, "We'll be feeding in about fifteen minutes but Helena's appetite is not what we would like it to be."

"Do you want to walk around until they feed?" Antony asked.

"She will have to move to her left to get away from the side of the tank. Let's wait and see what she does."

They sat on a bench behind the railing.

"If not for you, she would still be in danger," Antony said.

"She seems more miserable here than she was when dragging that crab trap around."

Antony twisted on the bench toward Minnie, putting one arm behind her. His knee brushed hers and Minnie almost shifted away from the touch. His anxiety was so evident that it seemed to take the form of an aura. She felt herself pressured to acknowledge him, and it made her uncomfortable.

"Each time we visit she will look better." His voice became animated as he attempted cheerful conversation. "I remember, the day we first saw her, how you ordered me out of the boat to make that phone call. And, when I returned, I couldn't believe my eyes. During the trip you had been almost afraid to move for fear of tipping over, yet there you were, standing up in the boat."

She felt his breath on her cheek, but she couldn't turn, couldn't look at him at such close range.

"I think I'd have jumped in if I could swim."

"You know, there's a place where they allow you to swim with manatees."

"I think it's too late for me to learn."

"Invite me over to the pool and I'll teach you."

"And set all the tongues wagging about us being together?" Minnie regretted the sting in her voice. It was only a manifestation of her own confusion, but it came out harsh.

Antony removed his arm from behind her and faced straight ahead. She knew she had wounded him.

"I'm going for a Coke," he said.

She watched him until he disappeared around a corner. Minnie stood and leaned on the railing. Even though his attentions today set her on edge, she didn't want to think of losing Antony's friendship. Yet it seemed to be slipping away.

The other two manatees had begun to swim in circles; perhaps they anticipated their dinner. The rippling water teased at Helena's skin, but she did not move.

Minnie And The Manatees

What would people say if she and Antony were together on a regular basis, Minnie wondered. Would they think less of her if they thought she was taking him back? Would she think less of herself if she did? Minnie blinked. That was the first time she had been conscious of seriously considering it. Was she weakening in her old age? Early on she had been devastated to think of him turning to another woman for pleasure. But lately there were days when his short-lived indiscretion seemed more like folly than cruelty. It had been a stupid thing, but not calculated. Hurtful, but not crippling.

Minnie forgot herself as Helena opened her eyes. The other two manatees were churning the water now, stretching their rubbery snouts as far as possible in the air. The female attendant approached the far side of the tank, pulling a wagon with high sides. Taking large clumps of seagrass with both hands, she scattered vegetation on the water. Minnie had once known what manatees ate, but could remember the names of only two plants because they had some familiarity: mangrove leaves and water hyacinth.

Helena's body twitched. Minnie saw her left flipper move in the water, which only pushed her more tightly into the side of the tank. She snuffed and raised her head. Then she sank below the surface, twisted, and was propelled toward the food by her tail, while lying upside down.

"Good girl," Minnie said.

The attendant looked across the tank at Minnie and gave her a thumbs up. Minnie watched Helena eat for several minutes, then went in search of Antony.

He was standing near the exit, soda in hand. "You missed it," she said. "Helena's eating."

"I'm glad," he said. "Are you ready to leave?"

Neither of them spoke as Antony pulled onto the highway and picked up speed. The top was down and hot air buffeted behind their heads. "Do you want the radio on?" he offered, when the silence became awkward.

"Do you really think you could teach me to swim?" Minnie asked.

Antony concentrated on the traffic. "It was a foolish idea," he said. "Unless, of course, you can find a pool where no one in the world would see us."

He parked in the lot at the condo and waited while Minnie got out of the car. When she closed her door he looked at her, his face softening a bit. "Take care of yourself, Min," he said.

He drove away before she even started moving toward the building.

As she set the dead-bolt, her home echoed with a new emptiness. She knew he would not be calling her for a while and she was already missing the ring of the phone.

Eager to be out of the lonely condo, Minnie sloughed off her shoes, slipped into flat sandals and headed for the grocery store. She walked the

Minnie And The Manatees

aisles, head down, avoiding people. So far she had not crossed one thing off her list but had picked up chips, a sour cream dip, bite-sized Milky Ways and a six-pack of Diet Pepsi.

"Hey, Minnie," she heard, then a shopping cart pulled up beside hers.

Marge Higgins had never looked so good. A loud paisley scarf wrapped her hair, long ends trailing down her back. But the orange and green colors almost paled beside the glow of her skin. Minnie cringed as each checked out the contents of the other's buggy. Marge's held both spinach and broccoli.

"How have you been, Minnie?" she asked. "Haven't seen you for a while."

Minnie wished for lipstick. "I'm fine. You're looking good."

"I've been seeing Ronald McKay," she spouted, unable to wait long enough to work it decently into the conversation.

"He's a nice man," Minnie answered, reminding Marge who had been on the scene first.

"You coming to the potluck tonight by the pool?" Marge asked.

"I'd forgotten. Probably not."

Marge pushed past her. "Well, see you around," she said.

I've been seeing Ronald McKay? It hadn't been that long since Minnie had asked Ronald to try to get to know Marge. Her statement seemed to indicate they had enjoyed several encounters already.

Minnie stuck her list in her pocket and headed for the checkout. She had more than she would need for this evening.

28

"To hell with it," Minnie said, tossing the magazine. Pages flared as it fell to the bedroom floor. Her herbal tea had gone cold, and she could not concentrate. Even the diet article had not held her attention. The finality in Antony's goodbye haunted her. Not so much the words but the dead tone of his voice. She had always feared their companionship would come to an end one day, but she thought it would happen when one of them found someone else. She hadn't anticipated that Antony might become weary of the tension and the testing. But it seemed that he had tired of wearing his heart on his sleeve only to have it ignored.

All her doors and windows were closed, and she could still hear the music from the potluck taking place below. Someone had brought a boom-box and an unending supply of salsa music. When not thinking about Antony she thought about Marge. No doubt Marge had reminded her about the potluck because she would be there with Ronald. Minnie could picture her in crinolines and those thick-soled, black tap shoes Spanish dancers wore.

Abandoning the hope of sleep, Minnie put on her robe and crept out onto the landing to look down at the pool. The only attempt at decoration was a long string of tiny white lights which stretched through the palms. But with the pool glowing turquoise and the poolside lamps lit, it seemed romantic. A couple of dozen tenants had broken into groups, some around the grill, some in lounge chairs and a few at the makeshift bar. Marge was easy to spot in a yellow jumpsuit with a Mexican sash at the waist. Also looped around her waist was Ronald's arm.

Suddenly Marge pointed up at her. "Look, it's Minnie," she shouted. "Come on down."

Minnie froze. The woman had to have the eyes of an eagle to have spotted her in the shadows. But then, she was Marge's favorite prey and probably Marge had been watching her door. Ronald looked up. Bridget Morris, who lived on the third floor, looked up. All Minnie could move was her right hand. She waved her fingers, like a baby. Henry Weinberg, who used to be part of her bridge group, called, "Good margaritas down here, Minnie." She dashed inside before anyone else could join the chorus.

There was no alternative; she had to go down. Anything else would broadcast that she was alone, and lonely. She put on her periwinkle blouse and long white skirt and a dash of makeup.

Minnie And The Manatees

As the elevator dropped, Minnie put her hand to her stomach. The Milky Ways and the Diet Pepsi were warring with the sour cream dip.

Henry Weinberg spotted her first and gallantly came to take her arm. "What kept you?"

"I had a bunch of phone calls," she said. Near to the truth. Earlier she had spoken to Antony's sister, Marie. And there was that young man with the offer for a home equity loan.

Henry dipped the rim of a plastic glass into a bowl of salt and poured her a pre-mixed margarita. Minnie spent a few minutes with him, fortifying herself, then squared her shoulders and sought out Ronald and Marge. Best to get it over with.

She found them at a dim edge of the gathering. Marge was teaching him a samba, or something equally seductive. No one else was even dancing. Minnie watched, trying to overcome her bias. They made a handsome couple, Marge's lithe body accenting Ronald's solid one. When she caught a good look at Ronald's face, she knew she had sent him on a mission from which she would get no information. He was grinning like a kid, freed from his normal reserve. Something had released him from his inhibitions and it didn't take a stretch of the imagination to guess what that might have been.

They finished the dance in a flourish, Marge giggling as Ronald spun her around. Minnie set her plastic glass on a circular wrought iron table and clapped. "Well done," she said.

Ronald came to such a quick halt that Marge spun past him.

"Minnie," they said in unison.

"I'm so glad you came down," Marge said, sidling closer to Ronald. "You looked so pathetic up there."

"Marge, please," he said, frowning at her.

"Oh, you know I don't mean it that way. My mouth always moves quicker than my brain." She said it as if that was an attribute. "It's just nice to have you here, isn't it Ronnie."

"Very nice. Can I get you a drink?"

Minnie retrieved her margarita. "I'm all set up." She met his eyes and felt him trying to convey a private message. What would it be? Maybe he wanted to say, I'm just doing what you asked of me. Or, I'm sorry I haven't called. Or, and this seemed most likely, I'm sorry, but I like her.

Minnie smiled at him. "You two make a striking couple. I'm glad to see you together."

Ronald's face relaxed. "Thanks, Minnie," he said, and she knew she had guessed correctly.

Marge started to pull at him. "Those burgers smell good. Let's get something to eat."

"Join us, Minnie?" Ronald asked.

"I ate earlier. I'll just sit here and finish my drink."

Henry came by again, then several neighbors stopped to chat, and when she looked around for

Minnie And The Manatees

Ronald she realized he had left without a goodbye. No doubt Marge had rushed him away.

She stayed until the end so she wouldn't have to listen to the music from upstairs. At five minutes past ten she fell into bed thinking of Marge and Ronald together. She was glad that he might have found the right woman, but Marge's influence could destroy a friendship she would dearly miss.

Had she lost the comfort of both the men in her life in one day? She was too exhausted to dwell on it for long. To avoid replaying the conversation with Antony, she concentrated on the happiness in Ronald's face. She fell asleep hoping that even accidental good deeds counted for something in the end.

29

Detective Wilkins combed his hair a half dozen times and changed his jacket twice. He couldn't figure out exactly what Catherine had intended when she called, but he was happy just to be seeing her again.

"Can you meet me on the Fort Myers pier?" she had asked.

"Sure. I'll even buy you a drink."

"We'll see," she replied.

Her voice had an edge to it, but he could think of no reason she would be put off with him. Their dinner had gone pretty well.

As he drove toward the pier anticipation took the place of apprehension. He wondered what she might be wearing, how her hair would be done. In a few weeks there was a policemen's benefit dance, a fancy affair. He intended to ask her to go with him. He pictured her on his arm, wearing a long sparkly dress. The guys at the station would fall all over themselves. That was the fun part of the fantasy. The part that made him swallow hard was knowing his feelings were deepening with each meeting. He wanted to know everything about her. What was her childhood like? What were her dreams? He wanted to take care of her.

As he pulled into the parking area he recognized Catherine's little sports car. He hiked along the pier, wishing he had thought to pick up a small bunch of flowers. Or maybe that would be too much. How was a guy supposed to know these things? By the time he spotted her he felt unsure again.

Catherine was at the end of the pier, her back against the rail, watching him approach. She wore white jeans and a silky shirt which sculpted her body when the breeze moved it just so.

"What a great day," he said, to avoid spitting out gushing compliments.

"I'm glad you think so," she snapped.

Wilkins stopped a few feet away from her. "Pardon me?" he said.

"Why have you been pursuing me?" She had not moved a muscle, and her face was a mask of control.

"I can't imagine you don't know the answer to that."

"Is it because of Mike?"

He saw flint in her eyes.

"No. But I do know a few things about Mike McCreary that makes me wonder why you are involved with him."

"Like the fact that he's married?"

Wilkins blinked, surprised. "He is?"

She smirked. "Some detective. His wife's name is Janice."

"It is?" He knew he was staring vacantly while his mind sorted out what she was saying.

Now she stood straight, not leaning into the rail. Her voice rose in frustration. "What's the matter with you?"

He moved to the railing so that they were nearer one another and she had to turn to look at him. He saw fine lines beneath the makeup and knew she had put on a cloak of toughness for this interview. She wanted to beat him at his own game.

He knew he was about to crush her, and that gave him pain. Holding her gaze, he said, "Janice McCreary is Mike's sister."

Catherine's body jerked. As Wilkins reached for her, afraid she might actually fall, she twisted away from him and put a hand on the rail to steady herself. She turned to face the gulf, both hands gripping the wood.

"That can't be," she said flatly.

"If they live together on Seashore Drive in Naples, they are brother and sister."

"How would you know that?"

"Unfortunately, the whole family is pretty well known among the local cops."

She stared at the water for several minutes while he studied her profile. Her mouth twitched occasionally, but otherwise she could have been

Minnie And The Manatees

a statue. Then she turned her head. Wilkins caught his breath when he saw the pure pain in her eyes.

"As they say in the movies, detective, that will be all for now. You're free to go."

He wanted to touch her, to comfort her, but sensed that she would spring at him like a wildcat for bearing such terrible news. "Will you be okay?"

"I said goodbye, detective."

Wilkins fought the desire to call her, knowing she would need time to absorb what he had told her. But, three days later, when duty took him near the Estero Shores complex, he pulled in beside the office. The car parked there was not hers.

A man with a neat white mustache and silver hair greeted him. Wilkins asked for Catherine.

"Ms. James is taking a short vacation. Can I help you with something?"

"No, just a friendly visit. When is she expected back?"

"I couldn't say."

While he drove back to the station, Wilkins called her twice. She didn't answer, and no machine picked up. Beginning to worry, he decided to visit her after his shift.

Back at his desk, he sorted through a dozen pieces of mail. A bulky manila envelope was addressed to him in flowing handwriting. He ripped it open and retrieved a small book. It was Catherine's weekly planner.

30

Wind whipped Ft. Lauderdale, making no distinction between multi-million dollar homes with matching yachts docked in the waterways behind them and decrepit shacks whose walls whistled from the blast. Catherine saw not one soul along the mile or more of shifting beach that was visible from her hotel window. The wild-headed palm trees bobbed and weaved like kick-boxers. She clicked on the television and surfed for the weather channel. Sanibel Island would be better. She decided to leave the next morning and called the desk to let them know.

After a room-service lunch she tried her magazine again, with no success. She knew that getting dressed, putting on her makeup and venturing out would be good for her. But emotions had overruled common sense for days. Racing down the freeway toward Ft. Lauderdale, disjointed thoughts had pummeled her. Mike's bald-faced lies. His manipulation. And the worst—using Adrian to gain her compassion.

Marlene Baird

Now, her anger at Mike had waned to the extent she could explore anger at herself. How could she have been so naive? She was no teenager lost in puppy-love; she had known loving Mike was risky. Was it her pathetic insecurity that made her settle for half a relationship?

And here she was in a hotel room with no one even missing her. Because she thought Mike was married, she had not confided the affair to anyone but Minnie. And, ashamed, she had retreated from the few friends she had before meeting him. She could hide out for weeks and no one but Minnie would even miss her.

She now regretted sending her appointment book to Wilkins; a consuming desire for revenge had caused her to act irrationally. When Mike had said Wilkins was using her to get at him, that indicated to Catherine that Mike was guilty of something serious. Still, Mike's whereabouts were his own business and she should not have exposed him. But that bridge had been crossed; what information the police might glean from her book had no doubt been extracted by now.

The questions she wanted to ask Mike began to swim, again, in her head. "Why did you pretend to be married?" "How many other lies have you told me?" She could hear his pleading, "Aw, Cat . . ." and knew he would explain everything away in the guise of protecting her.

She was so deep into this imaginary conversation that the ringing of the phone made her jump. It could only be the desk clerk.

"Hello."

"Hi, Catherine."

"Detective?"

"Please don't hang up."

"I thought you had delivered all your bad news. Don't tell me there's more." His long silence frightened her. "You mean there *is* more?"

"May I come up?"

"Surely, you're not in the hotel. How did you find me?"

"If you ever want to really disappear, don't use a credit card."

"But you have no reason and no right to be tailing me. I'm not a suspect in anything. Or am I?"

"No. But I do have important information for you."

Catherine held the receiver against her thigh. Did she really want to know anything more? But if something had resulted from her supplying the detective with the appointment book, then she had to hear it.

"Give me five minutes."

When he knocked on the door she was waiting. Purposely, she had done nothing more than brush her teeth and pull on jeans and a bulky sweatshirt. But she needn't have worried about deflecting the detective's attentions; he glanced at her, then moved past her into the room, his face drawn and sober.

"Did you bring my book back?" she asked, following him. The room held a round table with two chairs, but Wilkins stood with his back to the window, and Catherine hoisted herself onto a corner of the bed.

"The detectives working on a drug case will be holding it for a while."

"Drugs? Mike would not be involved in drugs."

"Maybe not. I'm not working that case. Do you need your book?"

"I'm just not sure that giving it to you was the right thing for me to do. Have I put Mike in jeopardy?"

Wilkins hesitated.

"Spit it out."

"McCreary put himself in jeopardy. And the police would have been successful eventually, without that kind of help."

"Where is he now?"

"I hate to bring this news, but didn't want you to find it out while you were alone."

Catherine felt the oxygen leaving her brain. Dizzy from anxiety she thought, I've done this terrible thing and he's dead. Attempting to stand, she slid from the bed, then found her legs unable to hold her.

Wilkins grabbed her arm. "Sit down." He pulled out one of the chairs and put her in it.

"Where is he?" she repeated.

"McCreary is in jail."

Minnie And The Manatees

Catherine slumped in relief, dropping her head into her hands.

Neither spoke for several minutes. Wilkins moved to gaze out the window, perhaps to give her some privacy.

Catherine raised her head. "Can you arrange for me to visit him?"

Wilkins turned. "Don't you want some details?"

"I want to hear it from him."

Yesterday it had been the detective who couldn't look her in the eye, now it was Mike. The room, with cement walls and a few metal chairs and tables, would have been cold even without the air conditioning. Catherine folded the sides of the yellow cardigan across her chest. From the moment the guard had escorted him to the small table, Mike's eyes had remained cast downward to the gray table. She waited, and, slowly, he brought his head up. Catherine looked into the face of the man she had loved for years. She knew the silkiness of those heavy brows, remembered the bristle of his chin which no razor had ever made smooth. But in his eyes there was something new. Sorrow was there, which she had seen before. Also, pleading, with which she was too familiar. The new element was fear. He had always been as solid as cement; now he was crumbling. She wanted to stay angry, to punish him, but seeing him weakened softened her.

"How much do you know?" he asked.

"I know you lied about Janice. I don't know why you are here."

He seemed in no rush to enlighten her, his gaze searching her face. Surely he didn't hope to find forgiveness.

"Who is Adrian's mother?" Catherine asked.

Mike drew in a breath that expanded his chest, then slumped back into his submissive attitude. "I never actually said I was married to Janice."

"Never actually said?" she exclaimed. Her voice went shrill, then she lowered it. "I'm sorry if I can't remember every word of every conversation. You certainly led me to believe it. As much as it hurt me, you let me believe it." She glanced at the half-windowed door to see if her outburst had alerted the guard. Then she repeated, almost hissing, "Who is Adrian's mother?"

"She left immediately after he was born. Janice moved in with me to help out. I got a divorce a year later."

Catherine leaned into the back of her chair to distance herself. If he was telling the truth now, which was impossible to judge, all this time he had been free to marry her. It didn't matter why he had refused; the knowledge that he didn't want her as a wife would always haunt her. But what was the point in going down that road now? She would recover, was recovering, and he was facing . . . she wasn't sure.

"Why are you here?" she asked.

Minnie And The Manatees

He seemed relieved to move on. "Cat, we don't have much time, but I want to start at the beginning."

She nodded.

"I've loved you since we first met, I will always love you."

"Please."

He waved a hand as if impatient with himself. "Okay, so much for my defense. You know now that I've told you many a lie. One just led to another. I'd have said anything to keep you in my life."

"Why couldn't I have been in your life without the lies?"

"When I told you about my early days in juvenile hall I was only describing the beginning. My entire family has been knocking against the law all our lives. And I have a reputation as a tough guy." He watched her as if judging whether she was getting his message. "A guy who takes care of other people's little problems."

Catherine recoiled, crossing her arms over her chest.

He hurried to reassure her. "No weapons, no breaking of fingers, just some muscle and threats. That was always enough."

"Until this time."

"An acquaintance offered me a good chunk of money."

"Wait," Catherine said, looking toward the door. "What if someone hears you?" Why she automatically acted to protect him was a mystery to her. Perhaps she could not accept that a man she had loved, had taken passionately to her bed, was a criminal.

"I've told them everything. Anyway, there was a punk involved in this drug operation, who didn't want to follow the rules."

"Drugs? Mike, how can you tell me this. Those drugs go to children, even children like Adrian."

"No, no," he said. "I had nothing to do with the operation itself, never have. God knows I've learned, through watching Janice, the devastation they cause. No, they just wanted me to talk to this guy and straighten him up a bit. He was just an intermediary, but he was getting cocky, too big for his britches."

Mike rubbed a fist against his mouth. "He was too stupid to listen, gave me nothing but lip. A real dick. We met, south of Tampa, on an abandoned floating dock. One of those that is enclosed on two sides, with a roof. From the moment he arrived, revving his boat and sloshing water over my shoes with the wake, I knew he was going to be trouble."

"Did you think twice about what you were doing?"

"Hu-uh. When you grow up like I did you learn not to. Anyway, we argued, then he threw a punch at me. I couldn't believe my eyes, such a runt. Like I said, no brains. Anyway, he wouldn't let up, and we ended up in a real fist fight. When he pulled a knife from inside his boot, my blood boiled and I hit him hard. He folded into a corner and didn't move." Mike seemed to be sorting his words, wondering how much more to say. "I'll just tell you it was ugly. A jagged piece of weathered dock was sticking up at a forty-five degree angle. He fell on it and cut his throat." Mike looked back down at the table.

Catherine couldn't help touching her own throat. She leaned toward him. "God, Mike, is it murder?" she whispered.

With his head still bowed, he said, "Manslaughter."

He was facing prison, and she may have hastened his capture. As he continued, Catherine felt grateful that he seemed unaware of her complicity.

"I put him back in his boat, set the throttle on low, and headed it south."

The door opened and a guard stuck his head in. "Two minutes," he said, then retreated.

"It's so gruesome," Catherine said. "Did you even know his name?"

"Simm."

Catherine blinked. "Jimmy Simm?"

"That sounds right, Jimmy Simm . . . the stupid punk. Surely you didn't know him?"

"He owned one of the condos." Catherine felt blood draining from her face. She recalled her interview with Detective Wilkins when he had insinuated that she was the only one benefiting from the deaths at Estero Shores. In fact, Mike had inadvertently handed her that commission. Catherine shuddered.

"What's wrong?" Mike asked. "You've gone pale."

Catherine shook her head to clear it. "It's just a shock. I remember reading about Simm's death. It was reported as a drowning."

"I was watching the papers for details, too. All I can guess is the cops weren't prepared to show their hand."

They sat in silence for a few minutes then she nodded toward the guard outside the door. "You said you told them everything. Why?"

"Janice has often lied to give me an alibi; they threatened to charge her as an accomplice. I don't know if it would have held, but we have a history of getting off pretty easy, and they're ready to stick it to us. So I bargained, but she may still get some time. They'll come up with impeding the investigation or something."

"But, what about Adrian?"

Tears welled in Mike's eyes and he didn't check them. "That's the worst part. Probably a foster home until Janice is free. Even then, who knows if they'll find her fit to care for him."

Surprising herself, Catherine said, "What about me? Could I take him?"

"Cat, that would be great of you. But, being connected to me, I don't think you'd have a chance."

He was no doubt right.

During all these years with Mike she had not allowed herself to even fantasize about having children and had not let herself admit, until this moment, that she wanted to be a mother.

Mike rubbed his wet eyes with the back of his hand.

Catherine stood.

He looked up at her. "You see why I couldn't offer you the McCreary name. I couldn't bring you into our lifestyle. You wouldn't have stayed."

"Love can do odd things, Mike. But I think you're right, I wouldn't have."

"Will you come visit me again?"

She shook her head.

He tried to smile. "You'll always be the best, Cat."

Marlene Baird

31

Antony's gaze rested on a trawler headed home for the night. He was parked on a sandy pull-out just large enough for one car. It was his favorite spot for watching the sun go down. Out of the last four nights, only a single sunset had proven spectacular and he preferred the duller ones. On those evenings he regretted less that Minnie could not share the moment with him.

    He pondered life without her. He knew it was human nature to move on. In most cases, after a long enough separation, both parties would lose interest and find someone else. He could readily see Minnie doing this, but saw no relief for himself. He'd had many opportunities with other women in the past few years. Beautiful women, generous women, all of them possibilities. But not one had even come close to changing his mind about Minnie.

    He wanted desperately to ask about the other man, but pride kept him from opening his mouth. Pride and fear. What if she said, yes, it was getting serious? He was ready to lay his life at her feet, promise and deliver on anything. But what would convince her he was serious? What could he offer up?

When the trawler disappeared behind buildings off to his right, he noticed a fine layer of dust on the pink hood of the car. For the first time in memory, he let it be.

32

Minnie called the president of the condo association, Peter Green.

"Peter, how would I reach the developer?"

"Minnie, if you have a problem, the place to start is with the association."

"No, it's nothing like that. Catherine James missed an appointment with me and the fellow taking her place has no information as to her whereabouts. I know that she lives alone, not in the best neighborhood, and I'm getting a bit concerned. I can't get a phone number for her, so I thought I'd ask her boss what he knew."

"She's no doubt taking a deserved vacation, but if you're worried, call Brian Goodings."

Minnie jotted down the number. "By the way, Peter," she said, "when we have these potlucks, aren't there rules about music and noise?"

"Reasonable activity until ten o'clock. You know that."

Minnie And The Manatees

"I don't consider three hours of salsa music to be reasonable activity."

She felt his hesitancy before he spoke. "Do you want me to make a formal complaint at the board meeting?"

Minnie pushed her glasses, hard, against the bridge of her nose. What was she turning into? A lonely, complaining divorcee, jealous of other people's fun?

"No. Don't do that. I withdraw the complaint."

Brian Goodings explained that Catherine had taken a week off, sounding aggravated that she had given him such short notice.

"You're darn lucky to have her, you know," Minnie said, hanging up.

At ten o'clock the next morning Catherine walked into the shop, and Minnie immediately waved her over. She had just started working on Valerie Germond and was already tired of the woman's whining.

"Hi, Catherine. I'm so glad to see you."

Catherine had on slacks and flat shoes. Minnie had never seen her out of her work clothes or her jogging outfit. She looked softer and even more beautiful.

"Minnie, I just realized this morning that I missed an appointment. I'm sorry about not calling."

Marlene Baird

Valerie Germond looked Catherine up and down, then cleared her throat, reminding Minnie that this conversation was interrupting her own. Minnie smiled at her then spoke to Catherine. "I'll bet your nails need attention. I can get you in tomorrow evening."

"That will be fine, but I really need to talk to you in private, as soon as possible."

The urgency in Catherine's voice made Valerie Germond look up at her, pencilled eyebrows arching like the McDonalds sign.

"I'm free at lunch," Minnie said.

"I'll come back and get you."

Catherine was only a few feet away, heading toward the door, when Valerie said, "Who was that?"

"Tell me again, was it Christopher or Pooh who chewed up that silk pillow?" Minnie asked, and Valerie was off.

Catherine drove a sports car, five or six years old, about the age of Minnie's car.

"This is so cute," Minnie said, partly to deflect her effort at ducking down to clear the door frame.

"Can we just pick up some drive-through, Minnie, and sit in the car?"

"Sure."

With no more conversation, Catherine drove a few blocks and pulled up to the speaker at Burger King. She ordered a fish sandwich on wheat and iced tea. Minnie copied her, wishing for a cheeseburger and fries.

Minnie balanced their bags and drinks on her lap, expecting Catherine to drive away. Instead, she simply wheeled around the building and parked in the lot.

"Well, this is scenic," Minnie teased, handing Catherine's lunch to her.

"I know you don't have much time, Minnie, and I've got quite a lot to say."

"You sound serious. Is there a problem?"

Catherine told Minnie, in detail, about breaking off with Mike, then learning that he had lied to her about being married.

Minnie nearly choked on a bite of her fish sandwich and her voice came out squeaky. "I can't believe it. Why would he lie about something like that?"

"That's a long story, for later. I was so angry with Mike, so hurt, that I gave Detective Wilkins ammunition against him, information that probably put him in prison."

Minnie sucked in her breath in surprise. "Prison? What for?"

"You won't believe that part of it, but that's not what I want to talk about just now."

"My goodness, it's more important than that?"

Catherine put her unopened sack on the floor behind her seat and took a sip of tea. She gripped the paper cup with both hands. "Minnie," she said, "I have the most impertinent favor to ask of you. In fact, it is so much more than a favor, I hardly know how to express it." Her eyes glistened with moisture and some secret.

Minnie folded the last bites of her sandwich in the paper and stuck it in the bag, dropping it to her feet. "Why so serious? You know I'd do anything for you. Anything I'm capable of."

Catherine chewed on her lip before continuing. "I'll give you all the details when we have more time, but Mike thinks Janice will do some jail time, too. That will leave Adrian alone."

"Oh, dear," Minnie said.

"I told Mike I would take him, but he intimated that if my background is checked and I'm connected to Mike I wouldn't stand a chance. All I've thought about since is finding someone to look after Adrian, someone the authorities would approve."

Minnie's drink was suspended between her lap and her open mouth. She turned in her seat. "Are you suggesting what I think?"

"You've told me how you love kids, wish you'd had your own. Once you came to mind, I could think of no one else." Catherine smiled. "Minnie, you'd be perfect. He looks like such a sweetheart in his pictures. I don't know how hard it is to qualify as a foster parent, maybe it would be easier if you were married, but they'd never find a better person."

Catherine went on, but Minnie barely heard her. Could she have a child to care for this late in life? The possibility had never occurred to her before. She allowed herself to imagine a child's hand gripping hers—the curled fingers, the smooth skin, the sweaty palm. She pictured a young face turned upward, asking for understanding and guidance. Then she felt a warmth spread inside her, and her upper body seemed to expand as if making room near her heart. She thought she might puff up and spill out the window of the little car. "Look at that funny woman," children would say, pointing and laughing.

Catherine had stopped talking and was staring at her. "What is it, Minnie? Have I frightened you?"

Minnie realized her right hand was pressing against her heart. She let it fall to her lap. "Maybe I should be frightened, but I'm not. Catherine, you may have just given me the greatest gift of my life. I wonder if the state puts children in the care of single women in their fifties?" Minnie realized she would be devastated if they didn't.

"Let's find out," Catherine said, starting the car.

33

Catherine sorted through the newspapers spread on her bed, tossing out the sections she knew she would not get to. She had been neglectful of the news lately, her thoughts too scattered to concentrate. Her arms collapsed on the pile that was forming in her lap as she remembered a recent call from Minnie. She smiled. Every time she thought of Minnie she smiled. Following their conversation about her possibly caring for Adrian, Minnie had bloomed like a flower unfolding in time-lapse photography. Color suffused her face, she moved faster, her voice carried more life. They talked often as Minnie kept Catherine updated on the procedure to become a foster parent so that Catherine could share the process.

She reached for another section of a paper, then quickly tossed it aside. Headlines about a drug ring. Each time Catherine thought about Mike her mind went fuzzy. Too many conflicting emotions. The one she wanted most to sustain, anger, seemed the most fleeting. She was seeing Mike through different eyes, through her own childhood unhappiness. Every time she walked into her house of late she was reminded how desperately she clung to lost hope. There sat the same kitchen table at which she had eaten lonely breakfasts, draped with the same cloth. Catherine had embroidered the daisies on the corners in hopes of pleasing her mother, and her mother had barely noticed.

It was time to sell the house and the furniture, time she gave up on finding comfort within these walls. It would be hard. But how much harder would it be for someone like Mike to turn his life around? He had been raised in an atmosphere of careless disrespect for the law. Lying was required for survival. He had said he hoped his son would be the one to break the pattern. He looked forward to educating his son, having him rise in the community and bring respect to the McCreary name. But that imagined son became Adrian. Dear, sweet Adrian. And her thoughts shifted again.

At ten-thirty the next morning Catherine was dusting the window sill at the sales office when a florist's delivery truck pulled up outside. A young woman entered carrying a long, narrow box.

"Are you Catherine James?" she asked.
"Yes."

The woman handed her the box. "Have a nice day," she said.

"This looks like a good start," Catherine replied.

Six long-stemmed coral roses lay among some greenery and baby's breath. Catherine pulled the tiny card from its envelope.

I hope this helps to make up for my bringing so much bad news. Dave Wilkins

Catherine lifted one stem and touched a perfect petal. Dave Wilkins was uncomplicated. He liked her. Though she hadn't believed it at first, because she didn't know of Mike's activities, Wilkins had her interests in mind when he injected himself into her life. She hadn't made it easy for him, and here he was apologizing.

Catherine returned the rose to its bed and picked up the phone.

"Hi, Minnie. Would you have a vase suitable for long-stemmed roses? I have nothing here at the office."

Minnie chuckled. "From Detective Wilkins, right?"

"Yes. And they're beautiful."

"I'll be right there."

Minnie brought the perfect vase. Tall and narrow, in cut crystal. "This is lovely," Catherine said, taking it from her.

"A wedding present from one of Antony's sisters. It held anniversary flowers for thirty-three consecutive years. And I don't think Antony ever missed a birthday. Certainly not a Valentine's Day."

Minnie smiled, but Catherine saw a glint of something besides happy memories in her eyes. "Do you still see him occasionally?" she asked.

"Not for a while."

"What happened?"

"I'm not sure." Minnie shrugged. "Just timing, I guess." She took the vase from Catherine. "We had better get these beauties into some water. This way to the restroom?" she asked, starting down the hallway.

"Yes," Catherine said.

Minnie was gone for several minutes. When she returned her smile seemed forced but she kept her voice light and teasing. "If I were you, I'd be calling this young man. The least he deserves is a thank-you." She handed Catherine the vase. "I need to get going."

Catherine arranged the flowers then crushed the box and stuffed it into the trash can. She carried the bouquet to her office, clearing a space on the corner of her desk. After looking up a number in the phone book, she dialed.

"Wilkins," he said, after she was transferred to his extension.

She heard the clatter of a busy office behind him. "It's Catherine. The roses are lovely."

"Beauty begets beauty," he said. "Was that Shakespeare?"

She laughed. "I never heard the expression before, but then I don't know much Shakespeare."

"Me neither."

If there was such a thing as a pregnant pause, this was it, Catherine thought. Then they both spoke at once, so everything was garbled.

She stopped abruptly, and Wilkins spoke more loudly. "Will you go to a charity ball with me? It's a week from Saturday."

Catherine hesitated.

"Are you checking your calendar?"

"No. I'm sure it's clear. You just surprised me. I had anticipated, maybe, a quiet dinner invitation."

"That would be great, too. But I've had this fantasy that keeps me awake nights. Do you own a long sparkly dress?"

His eagerness was childlike, but so honest. She sensed that if he ever lied to her about something important his eyes would cross. "I could probably find one," she said.

"I've been seeing blue. Do you like blue?"

"I think I'll surprise you."

"It won't be the first time," he said. "But this time I'll look forward to it."

34

Minnie couldn't believe the amount of paperwork involved in her application process. Though the forms did not actually spell it out, she sensed she would stand a better chance if she were married and younger. But she took heart in the fact that she was in exceptional health and was not looking to take in young children. If she wasn't lucky enough to be given Adrian, who was just one among the thousands of waiting children, she wanted to help someone about his age because she remembered the crushing insecurity of her own early teen years.

The questions on the forms dug deeply into her life, but with each answer she was grateful for her placid and straight-forward existence. There were no skeletons hunkering anywhere, just a history of a quiet life lived within the bounds of convention. She was in no way exceptional, and she hoped that in itself would help.

Few things distracted her. Occasionally she was reminded that the phone was quiet, that Antony had not called. This saddened her, making her turn more resolutely to her task. And the arrival of a postcard from Ronald made her pause. It bore a picture of the Eiffel Tower.

Minnie, this city is incredible. I don't recall asking if you had ever been here. When we are saturated with art and food, Marge shops and I walk. Because of your generosity, you have changed my life. Ronald.

Minnie attached the postcard to her refrigerator with a palm tree magnet. Generosity? In his happiness, Ronald had converted a request to make him a spy into an act of kindness. She touched the card with her index finger, then touched the finger to her lips. She might never know for sure who had made that phone call, but her ugly experience had somehow morphed into someone else's joy. Just as Mike's predicament had spawned her renewal.

As the authorities dissected her over a period of weeks, the flush of anticipation was often followed by the sucked-in breath of doubt. If they didn't want her . . . She couldn't finish the thought. She *would* succeed.

Seeing herself as useful and needed infused Minnie with an urgent strength. She began to walk regularly and was surprised at how soon she desired to go longer distances. As her body tightened, her mind sharpened. Vigor claimed her; she no longer required more than a few hours' sleep a night. Now she rose at sunrise, not because she was fretful but because she was anxious to explore every minute of the new day.

She approached Sylvia one morning after the water aerobics class. "Sylvia, you know what a klutz I am. Do you think you could teach me to swim?"

Failure was a word Sylvia apparently never contemplated. "Absolutely," she said without hesitation. "Come a half hour before class on Thursday."

After the first two sessions Minnie was elated at her progress. She could float at complete ease. No doubt those extra pounds on her hips and thighs were a help. She could lie flat back in the water, her arms and legs limp. Amazingly, the water sifted harmlessly into her ears. It fanned her hair, licked at her forehead and the edges of her eyes. Looking straight up, the sky was cut by tree limbs and the rise of her building. She could have lain still, watching the clouds forever, but Sylvia gave her not a moment's reprieve.

On only the third lesson she was crawling through the water, splashing and gasping.

"You have to submerge your face," Sylvia admonished. "Otherwise your neck will tire, and you will never be able to move smoothly through the water."

"I know. I know," Minnie said. How many hours had she watched Olympic swimmers? Their long, lean bodies. How they slipped into the water. Their oneness with the element which terrified her. She watched out of admiration and jealousy.

On the fifth day she managed to sink her face into the water and blow out through her nose. She took three strokes then hoisted her head and gulped a breath. Head back in the water, she took three more strokes followed by a gulping breath on the other side. After putting several of these together, she felt like a mermaid.

"Your kicking is sloppy," Sylvia shouted.

Minnie knew this because occasionally her ankles knocked one another and sometimes, while concentrating on breathing and stroking, she forgot to kick at all. Perhaps Sylvia did not understand that when one conquers a life-long fear, style is not a factor.

One morning as she poured over her answers on a new form, desperate for everything to sound right, Antony called.

"Hi, Min."

She hadn't heard his voice in so long it stunned her into silence. Then she sobbed, a gulping helpless sound.

"What is it?" The instant concern in his voice, the trueness of it, made her sob again. She realized how much she missed him, and it was a shock. Perhaps if she had not been embroiled in her project she would have been more aware of the loss. Throwing herself into the application process had been a joy, but had it been an escape too?

Minnie And The Manatees

And there was something else; pride had kept her from calling him. She had stuck her chin in the air and refused to share her momentous decision with the one person in the world she wanted most to hear it.

She wiped her nose and coughed to clear her voice. "I'm having a menopausal moment," she said.

"Still?"

"Don't be mean. It's a holdover, I guess. I'm all right now."

"How have you been, generally?" he asked.

"I'm undergoing a major life overhaul. You'd be proud. If you want to come over tomorrow night, I'll tell you all about it."

"Well, that's a surprise. I didn't really think you would want to see me."

"I'm sorry if I hurt your feelings that day we visited Helena at the sanctuary. For some reason I was feeling pressured. Please come over."

There followed an uncomfortably long silence.

"Antony?"

"I'm a little busy. Can we make it Saturday?"

Minnie was taken back. It was only Tuesday. Always, Antony had come to her at the first chance.

"Of course, if that's better. I'll make dinner."

Well, things change, she told herself, replacing the receiver. But his hesitancy nagged at her all day. By the time she got into bed that night fear pricked at her. What had prompted his call? She had been so surprised at her reaction to his voice, so eager to share her news, she had not thought to ask. Did he have news of his own to share? Maybe he was leaving the area. Or, could he be sick? The thought of another woman haunted her too, though she doubted he would have called to tell her that. Tired of wrestling with the bedding, she got out of bed at two o'clock in the morning and watched old movies until six. Cary Grant, Clark Gable, always in the same story: you can't see love when it's staring you in the face.

Minnie's Saturday schedule was full, with clients from ten o'clock in the morning to four-thirty. She worked automatically while her mind planned dinner. She hoped the mounded meringue on the lemon pie was holding its shape. At first it had seemed blatant to prepare Antony's favorite dessert, then she asked herself when she was going to stop playing games. There were certain things she wanted in her life. A child was one, and she was doing her best to make that happen. Why not be honest and admit that she wanted Antony if it could be on her terms: she missed his company, and she wanted his support in her parenting venture.

Her client, Gladys Smith, a three-year customer and friend, said something. Minnie looked up.

"You're miles away," Gladys said.

"I'm sorry. Lots going on in my life right now. I'm contemplating a major decision."

"About a man?" she asked.

"Partly."

Gladys' voice went soft. "Wasn't it so much easier when we were young, before life knocked us around. We didn't have the sense to be cautious."

Minnie remembered her first date with Antony. Nothing in the world could have convinced her he wasn't the most wonderful man on earth. "I had such a romantic notion of marriage. I expected uninterrupted devotion and affection. This time I'll settle for respect and mutual support."

Gladys took her hand from Minnie's. "Surely you haven't given up on love, on passion?"

"I don't really want to do that again, surrender myself. I think a bit of distance this time. A buffer zone."

Gladys presented her nails for completion. "I hope that's not true, Minnie. It won't work if you hold back."

Gladys's admonition stayed with Minnie through the afternoon. She recalled the day, sitting in Catherine's little car talking about Adrian, when her heart had almost split open because it was so eager to envelop another person. Was there room there for all of Antony, not just the safe part?

Marlene Baird

As she showered and dressed for dinner she rethought her motives. She had missed Antony's companionship and hoped that tonight their friendship could be restored. She had not allowed herself to consider whether or not she missed his loving, or whether or not it could be anything like before. As she slipped into a pair of slacks that hadn't fit for two years, Minnie realized she had been wrapped up in what Antony could do for her. What was she willing to risk for his happiness?

By seven o'clock, the time Antony was expected, Minnie had changed her blouse, removed her earrings and was weary from indecision. So much would depend on how he approached her. If he was distant, and her hopes of recapturing him seemed too late, she could launch into the news about Adrian and hide her disappointment. But what if there was a real chance of them getting back together? Kids had never been a priority with Antony. During the marriage she knew he enjoyed not having to share her attentions. Back and forth she went, *he'll be happy for me and want to be a part of it.* Then, *it will distance us even further.*

She opened the door and almost sobbed again to see the face she had missed. His cheeks were glowing and his hair was mussed, no doubt from having the top down. One hand was in a pocket, from the other dangled a bottle of wine. He grinned like a kid, so clearly happy to see her that she blushed.

Minnie And The Manatees

He stood on the cement landing and stared at her.

"Well, come in for heaven's sake," she said.

"Minnie, you look so beautiful."

"I said, come on in." She left the door open and moved inside.

She heard the door close, then Antony rummaging in the kitchen drawer for the opener. She watched him pop the cork.

"My goodness, no twist top?" she teased.

"Are you supposed to let this stuff breathe?" he asked.

Minnie had no idea, but since she was having trouble breathing herself, she said, "Probably doesn't matter."

Antony half-filled two drinking glasses and brought one to her. He raised his. "To whatever good news it is you have to share."

The glasses clanged together.

They sat on the sofa and Antony took to studying her some more.

"For heaven's sake, Antony."

"You said that earlier."

"Well, don't stare at me."

His eyes went to the coffee table. "Okay, you talk and I'll just watch this magazine."

She pushed him playfully on the arm. "You know what I mean."

"Sure. Tell me about your new life."

"I'm swimming," she said.

"For God's sake. I never thought it would happen."

"I love it. There is such freedom in the water. I roll around under the surface and think of my manatee and her baby, and Helena."

"I went to see her last week," Antony said.

"I've been too busy to visit. How is she?"

"Not nearly so lethargic, and she can maneuver without that flipper just like a pro."

Minnie drank her wine, smiling. "We did good," she said.

The oven timer pinged, and Minnie rose.

"What smells so good?"

"Just a little pork roast," she said moving to the kitchen.

"Real gravy?" he called.

"Yes, real gravy. I'll be a few minutes getting things ready. Why don't you read that magazine."

He came into the kitchen. While she had both hands occupied lifting the roast from the pan with two forks, he brushed his lips against her cheek. Minnie almost dropped their dinner.

Antony refilled their glasses and carried his back to the living room.

After dinner he leaned back in his chair and sighed. "That was a wonderful meal, Min. The best I've had since your crab cakes."

"Want some pie?"

"Let's wait. I ate so much. I'd love some coffee, though."

Minnie And The Manatees

"It's set up. Just plug it in."

Antony started the coffee then went into the bathroom. Minnie looked at the table and his chair. There was a completeness in the scene—she and Antony and a shared meal. Then she pictured a child sitting with them. From his attentions it was clear that, if she chose, she and Antony would be together again. But she also knew that she wouldn't sacrifice the child to have that happen.

The moon hung full, so Minnie didn't turn on the patio light. Antony had helped her with the dishes, during which time they had not spoken about anything personal. The activity of cleaning up was welcome since the air seemed heavy with unexpressed thoughts. Minnie's tongue was bound by the fear that she might have to choose between Antony and a child. But she couldn't guess why he, too, had sobered.

"You've become rather serious," she ventured. "Are you tired?"

Antony stood, picked up his chair and set it down so that they were facing one another. When he sat, their knees almost touched. He took both her hands. "Minnie, I want you back. I need you."

The first statement did not surprise her; the second put her on guard. *I need you.* She wanted Antony's love, but she didn't *need* him. She realized with a jolt that even if Antony were to disappoint her again, it would not be as painful as before because she had filled her life with purpose.

"What exactly is it you need?" she asked.

"Your touch. Your voice. I need to see your face every day. These last weeks without any contact have been pure hell."

Antony reached into his pants pocket and produced a small velvet box. He held it out to her. It could only be a ring. Minnie studied his face trying to anticipate his intention, but he gave nothing away. She wanted the ring and all the possibilities that it presented. With a trembling hand, she pushed the box back toward him. "There's something you have to know."

"No, Min," he said. "It's yours. No strings." He flipped up the lid and removed the ring from its satin bed. A diamond solitaire scattered moonlight in a thousand directions. "Let me see it on you."

"You can't possibly afford this."

"Hush."

She slid it on. Antony didn't seem to notice that it went onto her right hand. "It's lovely," she murmured, turning it to catch the light. "But I know this cost thousands of dollars."

"I sold the car."

Minnie's hand dropped to her lap.

His eyes crinkled at the sides. "Didn't think I could live without it did you?"

"I once thought I'd be burying you in it. And there were times when that seemed like a real good idea."

The smile went out of his face.

"I'm sorry. I need to let that go. How did you get over here tonight?"

"I resurrected the Harley. That's why I couldn't come on Tuesday night. I needed time to get it fixed."

She looked into his eyes for a long time. "Antony, I—"

"It's okay. I mean it, no strings. I would love for you to consider it an engagement ring, but if not, it's a gift I should have given you long ago. I would do absolutely anything to have you back, but I respect that you might not be able to do that."

"You're sure you would do absolutely *anything* to have me back?"

"Yes."

"Let's go inside. I have a long story to tell you."

35

Antony injected surprise more than once while Minnie sketched the story about Catherine, Mike and Janice. It took a long time to fill in the details that led up to the likelihood of jail time for both the McCrearys. She didn't mention Adrian.

He sat still for a few moments after she stopped talking, then said, "You realize you helped to solve Jimmy Simm's murder?"

Minnie wrinkled her brow. "Oh, because I was the one who got Detective Wilkins interested in Mike. I never really thought of it that way. I've been more inclined to feel guilty about bringing Mike into it because Catherine had sworn me to secrecy. She and I have commiserated many a time about our involvement in Mike's capture. But Detective Wilkins assured Catherine that Mike would have been found out eventually, and we hold on to that."

"I'm sure the detective is right." Antony sat back on the sofa. "Well, that is a story, all right."

Minnie And The Manatees

"Oh, that's not the story," Minnie said, shifting closer to him. "That's the backdrop to the story."

He leaned forward. "I can't believe it gets more interesting."

"Mike McCreary has a son, a son with Down Syndrome. Mike's boy is named Adrian. He's fourteen years old."

Antony waited, his face blank.

"Adrian is going to need care if Janice is prosecuted. Catherine came to me and asked me if I would help."

"What about McCreary's family?"

"They're all bad apples. Mike thinks Adrian will be moved to a foster home."

Antony chewed his bottom lip. "And you want that foster home to be yours?"

"More than anything."

"Why do you think the authorities would give Adrian to you?"

"They may not. But what happened, when Catherine approached me . . ." Minnie shrugged. "I don't know how to explain it. The thought of having a child to care for, whether Adrian or someone else, consumed me. From that moment I've not been able to think of anything else."

Antony rubbed his palms together. "I think I see where I come in. You might consider having me back if I agree to support you in this."

"Not just support, Antony. Not a part-time thing. I want a real family." Minnie felt her body heating at the thought of she and Antony being together again; there was more than a slip of desire. She couldn't read his face, and she heard a hint of desperation in her own voice. "We might not be able to recapture what we had. Maybe it would be different. I wouldn't know what to expect."

He sat so still she wanted to shake him. He twisted the corner of his mouth as if in deep thought, then said, "I suppose I could put a sidecar on the Harley. Would he like that, do you think?"

It was impossible to know who had moved first but suddenly she was in his arms. The brush of his cheek on hers, the smell of his hair, everything was the same. Their hearts pounded together, their voices blended in muffled promises. After a few moments he drew back to look into her face. His eyes were soft, a smile at the corners. He rubbed her nose with his. "Remember the Eskimo kiss?"

Minnie opened her mouth to reply and he kissed her. The lips she knew so well pressed hers. He put one hand in her hair as he always had. She fell back in time, and the five lonely years became a moment.

36

The sofa pillows had been plumped a half-dozen times; the sliding glass doors were so clean one was tempted to walk through them. Still Minnie looked about for something that might be improved. She was reminded of her nervousness when she used to fear the police coming to her door. This time it was simply a social worker, but her anxiety level was almost as high.

There had been one perfunctory visit early on by a Mr. Kidmore, a young man with a pony tail, but he seemed to be simply taking the lay of the land. Since then she had filled in form after form and now faced her first in-depth, personal interview. Olivia Keene, the expected guest, sounded like a young girl on the phone, so Minnie had no idea what to expect.

When the doorbell rang Minnie took a deep breath, smoothed her blouse and raised her chin. Bad news would be too much of a blow; she had to put that out of her mind.

Mrs. Keene was probably Minnie's age, without the dyed hair or makeup. She wore a conservative skirt and jacket. She held out her hand and smiled. Pale green eyes met and held Minnie's. "So glad we finally meet face-to-face," she said.

"Yes," Minnie replied. "Come in."

As they moved through to the living room, Mrs. Keene remarked on how comfortable Minnie's home was, and Minnie didn't know whether that was just conversation or an assessment. She didn't reply, but motioned Mrs. Keene to her best chair and sat on the sofa. Minnie crossed her legs, then uncrossed them.

"Please don't be nervous Mrs. Zuccarelli. I bring more good news than bad."

That could only mean there was *some* bad news. Minnie swallowed a lump in her throat.

Olivia Keene opened her briefcase and put a file on the coffee table. Minnie knew her entire life was documented therein.

"First, some very good news," Mrs. Keene said. She paused just a moment. "I know you were particularly interested in Adrian McCreary."

The past tense of the verb registered with Minnie.

"You will be very happy to know that, if it becomes necessary, Adrian will go to a wonderful home." Mrs. Keene looked down at her file, giving Minnie a moment to absorb that. Then she continued. "A half-sister of Janice McCreary has asked for him, and, where possible, we prefer a child stay within the family."

"But—" Minnie began.

Mrs. Keene shook her head. "Don't say it. I know what you're thinking, but this is a home full of accomplished people who are more than anxious to give Adrian all the love and attention he will need. The half-sister and her husband have two boys. They live in Idaho and spend a lot of time doing outdoor activities. It is a perfect setting for Adrian."

Minnie stood and walked to her glistening glass doors, blinking away tears. She pulled a tissue from her pocket, dabbed at her eyes, and returned to the sofa.

"You know I'm disappointed," she said.

Olivia Keene knew how to handle emotion. She moved to the next point of business. "You emphasized in your application that you'd had experience with Down Syndrome. Is that really important to you, or was it important to you because of Adrian?"

"Even though I'd never met him, I felt a connection with Adrian, probably because I thought of him so often."

"The reason I ask, is that your age is against you becoming a foster parent for a Down Syndrome child."

"Why?" Minnie asked.

"You said in your application that you would prefer to take only one child, but keep that child as long as possible."

"That's right."

"If you were to take a normal teenager, that boy or girl would become an adult in a few years. By that I mean someone capable of looking after themselves. A Down Syndrome child needs care for as long as they live. You can see why the age of the foster parent is a consideration."

"I hadn't thought that through," Minnie admitted. "But I understand your position."

"So, what I need to know today, Mrs. Zuccarelli, is whether you are just as interested in a child with the usual health and emotional problems that most teenagers bring."

"Of course I am," Minnie said. "I knew my chances of getting Adrian were slim, but once I made up my mind to try, I knew that being a foster parent was my true goal. I would be grateful to take anyone who needs me."

Olivia Keene closed the file and put it back in the briefcase. "That's good news. We need people like you." She stood.

"But you have nothing concrete to offer me now?" Minnie asked, rising.

"I needed to clear up the situation with Adrian first, but I think you stand a good chance."

As they moved back toward the door Minnie knew she had a confession to make. "Mrs. Keene," she said, "I guess you would want to know if I were planning to marry again."

The woman stopped and turned. "That's important. Is this a recent decision?"

"Yes. But I know the man well. I was married to him for thirty-three years."

"If I may inquire, why didn't you stay together?"

Minnie's heart clunked in her chest. She had been so concerned about giving up Antony, if necessary, to keep Adrian. Now would she be facing giving up a child to keep Antony?

"He had a quick affair."

She watched Mrs. Keene's face. Only one eyebrow rose slightly. "That, alone, would not necessarily disqualify you as a couple. I'm sure there are innumerable indiscretions that we never learn of. However, bringing a new person into the picture will delay things. Your husband would need to go through all the hoops that you have. Do you think he is up for that?"

Minnie grinned. "We've talked about it and I know he will do whatever he needs to. He did one stupid thing in his life, but he has made up for it dozens of times. I'm more sure now than I ever was that we will have a solid marriage."

Mrs. Keene opened the door. "Get in touch after the wedding and I'll send some new forms. We live by forms."

"Thanks for coming," Minnie said. "And I am happy about Adrian."

The tears came later, spilling onto Antony's shirt. Minnie had come to know Adrian through Catherine's eyes, though neither of them had ever seen him.

"There are any number of kids who need you, need us," Antony said, pulling her closer.

"I know, and I'll love that child just as much as I would have loved Adrian."

37

Minnie called to Antony. "I've just performed an illegal operation."

He appeared in the doorway of the second bedroom where they had set up the new computer. Shaving cream covered half of his face. "What did you do?"

"Nothing bad. I just typed in 'foster parenting' and clicked on Search."

"You must have done something else. The guy at the class said the computer never lies."

"Well, what should I do now?"

He peered over her shoulder. "Try to cancel."

Minnie clicked on the Cancel button and the message disappeared.

"Well it lied that time," she said. "It said it was going to shut down and it hasn't."

This time the search engine brought up the first ten of several thousand possible connections.

Antony returned to his shaving, and Minnie tried a few websites. At FosterLove she found a story of a single mother who had helped to raise over three hundred children. The number was impressive, but Minnie hoped to have a child for a long enough time to really connect.

Antony reappeared, rubbing his face with a towel. "Shouldn't you be getting ready?"

"I only have to exchange this robe for my dress." She shut down the computer and moved to the master bedroom.

In the mirror she watched the lined satin slither over her body, falling to her ankles. Though excitement was bubbling inside, she looked like a column of cool water. She fixed a coronet of baby roses in her hair.

Minnie's eyes teared as the music swelled, and she tightened her grip on Frank's arm. Antony's sister, Marie, was standing up with her and Marie's husband, Frank, would give Minnie away.

"You look absolutely lovely," he said, pressing his shoulders firmly back. "No crying now. That's our cue."

They started up the aisle of the small church. Minnie sought out Antony standing up front, then everyone else rose and turned her way. Two of Antony's other sisters and their families had made the trip. There were nieces and nephews she hadn't seen in many years. Everyone from the beauty shop came, as well as friends from the condo. She passed Catherine and Detective Wilkins who were holding hands. Antony's buddies and their wives rounded out the thirty-five invited guests. As if the day weren't special enough, Marge Higgins had been forced to express their regrets since she and Ronald were going to be in Denver.

Frank left Minnie at Antony's side and the minister began the ceremony. Minnie tried to concentrate, but she was aware of Antony's heavy, shaky breathing. She looked at him. He kept his eyes forward but was blinking and tightening his mouth. She took his hand. He crushed her hand in his, and she knew he was pressing away tears.

Suddenly the minister was asking, "Antony Martin Zuccarelli, do you take Minnie Lynn Zuccarelli to be your lawfully wedded wife, to love and to cherish . . ."

Antony looked into Minnie's eyes. His hand relaxed from its tight grip, and the stress left his face. He pursed his lips and sent her a silent kiss. Then he winked. She thought he wasn't paying attention. But at exactly the right moment he said, "I do. Again and forever."

Find other books by this author
from the publisher, AuthorHouse
www.authorhouse.com
or order from your favorite bookseller

Following is a preview of Marlene Baird's
next novel, *Almost Home*
due in late 2004

ALMOST HOME

Prologue

The cover of the old family album, which contains the first pictures of me, has a pebbly, faux-leather finish. By the time I took an interest in it, its corners were frayed, showing the white fuzz of cardboard. Had I been older than eight or nine when I came across it, perhaps the false cover would have warned me that what was inside would also disappoint.

The first picture is of the three of us: two infants and a two-year-old. Bundled on the sofa and brightened by a shaft of sunlight, the twin babies glow like golden dolls. But the pale two-year-old stands in shadow. With the tip of one finger in her mouth, she frowns at the unfamiliar attention of the camera.

I remember studying the spine of the album to see if pages had been torn out and I had missed earlier photographs, but no. Had there been no pictures taken of me in my first two years which warranted mounting?

This evidence that my arrival had been unheralded pained me for many years. But now, with the advantage of time and distance, I feel a tug of forgiveness. My parents were very young. My mother went from leading her high school cheer squad, wearing a flirty skirt, to motherhood and shapeless maternity smocks. I can see how she might have resented me. Still, I was real, and I needed her.

Every picture of me includes the twins. They grow more and more beautiful, with bodies that naturally pose with grace. I exhibit a reserve and an awkwardness which I carry until college. In grade school I towered over my classmates, much too large, and at home became the opposite—invisible. Not all lonely children grow up to find their solace in drinking, so why did it happen to me? Is addiction in my genes, my burden from birth? Is there nothing I could have done to stave it off before it destroyed everything that mattered?

In my twenties, with years of drinking already behind me, there were moments when my breath would catch. I'd pass a mirror and see a person with dull eyes when I thought mine must be sparkling, or I would emit a raucous laugh which surely was not my own. I had a fear of losing control, but shrank from acknowledgement. I told myself I had the strength to flirt with disaster without suffering consequences.

Even at thirty-two years of age I was still positive I could avoid wreckage. It took the threat of the loss of my daughter to get me into the Jeep that day in late August.

About The Author

Minnie and the Manatees is Marlene Baird's third published novel. It was inspired by a visit to Florida where she became enchanted with the peaceful creatures represented in the story. In 2003 this book took first place in a nationwide contest sponsored by the Arizona Authors Association. Marlene lives in Prescott, Arizona with husband, Bob.

CPSIA information can be obtained
at www.ICGtesting.com
Printed in the USA
LVHW090947200321
681992LV00033B/294